Almost Abducted

A Kate and Doris Mystery

by

Trisha Durrant

For information, email **Cozy Cat Press**, cozycatpress@aol.com or visit our website at: www.cozycatpress.com

COZY CAT
P R E S S

ISBN: 978-1-946063-23-6

Printed in the United States of America

1 2 3 4 5 6 7 8 9 10

Many thanks to Susan, who volunteered to be my beta reader in the book's early stages. A big thank you to John, Gail and Steve for all the encouragement. And a huge shout out to my wonderful Mysterians writing group—not only for their insightful critiques of my work—but for the fun we have problem-solving over a glass of Battery Park Book Exchange's excellent wine and beer. Thank you also to our amiable host Tom, and the most congenial staff ever.

Prologue

The hot, humid air hung over the small Indiana town like a smothering blanket. The few people who braved the relentless sun beating down on the almost deserted streets scurried from one patch of shade to the next.

So only the old, black dog noticed the car. He had dug a cool spot for himself under the over-grown lilac bush on the front yard of the house opposite the small, red-brick office building. He had noticed the car a few minutes earlier as it made its slow careful way down the block. This time around, he watched warily as the white compact came into view again and pulled into the alley next to the building. A short stocky man got out, unzipped his light windbreaker, adjusted his heavy wrap-around sunglasses and moved swiftly to the office door.

The dog heard a sharp pop. Then, no more than twenty seconds later, another. He struggled slowly to his feet wondering whether or not to bark at the stranger who had so rudely interrupted his nap. Before he could decide, the door opened and the man came out. He got back into the car, pulled through the alley, turned left and headed towards the highway.

The old dog watched the car drive away, scratched irritably at the baked soil, turned around once, yawned and went back to sleep.

Chapter 1

"Look where the hell you're going, you stupid woman."

A horn beeped; there was a squeal of brakes and I almost bounced off the front end of an airport golf cart. It came to rest inches from my shaking body. The old man who yelled was clinging to the side rail, glaring at me. He had almost been ejected by the sudden stop. I took a deep breath, bit back the word I wanted to throw at him and plowed on through the slow-moving crowds, trying to dodge the screaming toddlers, baby strollers and wheelchairs that blocked the concourse of the busy San Diego airport.

Up until a few months ago I would never have cursed at anyone. In fact, my curse vocabulary was woefully deficient, bordering on non-existent, but I'd spent the last few hours on a crowded plane squashed between two loud, large men who talked over me the whole flight. I avoid alcohol while flying, but since I was inhaling whisky fumes from both sides I didn't think a Mai Tai would make much difference. I was wrong and had the headache to prove it.

I finally reached my gate for the last leg of my journey back to Indiana. It was deserted and the posted sign read, "two hour delay." A miserable ending to a miserable vacation, which I knew was going to be miserable so I had nobody to blame but myself.

At least, when I finally boarded the plane I had the row to myself. But just when I thought I was safe, a little old lady came trotting down the aisle. Her faded eyes peered anxiously at her boarding pass as she checked it against the seat numbers. "Please don't sit in my row," I said under my breath. "Please don't sit in my row."

She worked her way down the aisle—stopped—put her shabby purse on the aisle seat next to me and proceeded to hoist her vintage suitcase in the direction of the overhead compartment. She barely cleared five feet and no way could her skinny little arms get that suitcase over her head. I looked around, hoping someone else would come to her rescue, but everybody was too busy with their iPads and cell phones, and that left me. Blame it on all those years in Girl Scouts. I still remember raising my right hand and swearing to help other people at all times. I reluctantly got out of my seat, took the suitcase from her wrinkled hands, and stowed it in the overhead.

She sat down with a sigh of relief, patted her tight little gray curls back into place, and turned her gaze on me. "I'm Doris, Doris Weppler."

She looked at me expectantly, so I had to say, "Kate Conley." My head was pounding. I leaned back, closed my eyes and hoped she'd take the hint.

No such luck! Her quavering voice said, "Miz Conley, how do you work this dad-blamed seat belt? The thingie just won't go in here."

I opened my eyes. She was trying to hook two different seat belts together. I took the ends from her, fished down the side of the seat for the correct part, and snapped it together. The flight attendant came past and told Mrs. Weppler to put her purse under the seat. I grabbed it before she could ask me to unhook her and stowed it away.

"Did you come off the flight from Hawaii?" She pronounced it *Hu-why-yuh.*

The pounding in my head was getting worse. Reluctantly, I mumbled, "Yes."

Mrs. Weppler seemed delighted. "That's where I came from. Was it a vacation? Did you go by yourself? How did you like it?"

I muttered, "Fine," and leaned back to take another stab at trying to sleep. That's when the monster child behind me started to kick the back of my seat. I gave his mother a scathing look, which she totally ignored. Then the flight attendant stopped her cart at our row and asked what I wanted to drink. I shook my head which was a big mistake as the intermittent pain had now changed into a permanent throbbing ball of agony. The little voice next to me piped up, "We'll have two coffees with extra creamer and sweetener."

She leaned over and whispered, "Didn't you want any? We're paying for it, you know." I saw her stow the extra sweetener and creamer into her old purse. In spite of the headache, I almost laughed. My grandmother used to do the same thing. When we went out to eat all the sugar and sweetener packets on the table disappeared inside her purse. Grandma always told me we were paying for it and "they" left the packets on the table for us to take.

Doris, as she told me to call her, slid over next to me. She turned to the still kicking monster child, "You don't stop that I'll cut your legs off. Can't you see this lady is trying to sleep?" The mother gave a horrified gasp, but the kicking stopped. Doris talked the rest of the way back to Indianapolis.

When we landed, I retrieved her bag from the overhead. It seemed rude to stride ahead in the terminal so I carried it to baggage claim for her. I noticed her anxiously scanning the crowd.

"Is someone meeting you?"

"My cousin, Charlie, but he's not here yet. I hope he got my message."

"Why don't I call him for you?"

There was no answer from the cousin.

By this time, I'd plucked my bag from the spinning carousel and was ready to go, but I couldn't just leave her there alone—the Girl Scout thing again. A half-hour later, we were still there watching a lone suitcase going round and around the conveyor belt. The woman behind the car rental counter turned off her sign and hurried away. It looked as if everything was shutting down for the night. I tried calling her cousin again. There was still no answer.

I was more than ready to leave. "Doris, why don't you sit here? I'll check the ticket counter. Maybe he's waiting there."

I left her with the luggage and went upstairs. No cousin. When I came down the escalator, there was no Doris. Our bags were on the floor in front of the chairs where we'd been sitting, but she was gone.

I hurriedly checked the restroom. It was empty. The car rental counter was abandoned. The only other place was outside. I ran through the door and saw her across the street. A man was helping her into the passenger side of a white compact, but her skinny little arms were braced on both sides of the door, and it looked as if she were resisting.

"Hey, you forgot your suitcase!"

The man turned at the sound of my voice. Doris frantically pulled away and stumbled back into the line of traffic. She was almost hit by a black SUV whose driver honked and yelled at her. I darted across and grabbed her. She clung to me and I pulled her to safety onto the pavement outside the terminal's automatic doors. The man started after us. Doris stumbled towards the entrance. I hauled her inside and let the doors close.

He stopped and stared at me through the glass. His eyes were camouflaged by dark wrap-around sunglasses, but I could feel the menace in his stare. He moved towards the door.

I pulled Doris further inside, looking around for help.

"Are these your bags?"

I turned and almost collided with an officious looking man in airport uniform. He stood next to our luggage with an accusing look on his face.

"Yes, yes they are," I almost babbled with relief.

I heard the doors open, then close. Linking my arm through Doris,' I moved closer to our savior.

"Didn't you see the signs about not leaving your bags unattended?"

"Sorry, I wasn't thinking. We went outside to check if my friend's ride had come."

I looked back toward the entrance doors. The man hadn't come inside. He was still watching us through the window. He took one last stare, calculating, then ran back across the street to the car, jumped in and sped away.

An airport shuttle pulled up outside. We picked up our various belongings and hurried to catch it. I wasn't sure the security guard was going to let us leave. As it was, he walked us to the door and followed us outside, still not entirely convinced we weren't a couple of over-age terrorists, intent on blowing up the airport with a vintage suitcase bomb. He stood on the sidewalk in what he evidently thought was an intimidating pose, hands on hips, and watched until we boarded and the bus had left the curb.

I leaned into Doris. "Who was that man with the car? He wasn't your cousin, was he?"

She hesitated, then said, "No. I don't know who he was."

"He looked as if he were trying to kidnap you."

I saw the driver's head go up. He stared at us through his rear-view mirror. I lowered my voice. "We should call the police."

Doris grabbed my cell-phone to stop me. "No, it wasn't anything; he probably got me mixed up with somebody else." But her face had a grayish cast and her whole body shook.

We were the only passengers on the shuttle. When the driver dropped us off, he drove away slowly, still looking at us through his rear-view mirror.

And I was left in the middle of an almost empty parking lot with an old woman who didn't seem to have any place to go. It was getting late. We'd been on one plane or another since early morning and judging by the shabby purse and battered suitcase, Doris couldn't afford a hotel.

What could I do? Before I could stop myself I heard, "Doris, would you like to stay at my place tonight and we can get hold of your cousin in the morning?"

Her faded eyes filled with tears. She nodded yes. I paid the exorbitant parking fee, and we drove home to Shelbyville.

Chapter 2

I awoke to the smell of bacon and coffee. Staggering into the kitchen, I found Doris at the stove, cooking. She was dressed in the same clothes she'd worn the previous night, but with an apron now covering her dress, and fluffy slippers on her feet.

She smiled when she saw me, "You want some pancakes with your bacon and eggs?"

I did, even though I usually had a bagel and cup of tea in the morning. Dinner, which I found out later, was chicken and dumplings, was already simmering on the back of the stove.

"I'm going to make some slaw to go with that. I cleaned out your refrigerator and freezer, Kate. You had a lot of stuff going to waste."

She was right. I no longer cooked. I threw out whatever was too stale to use and bought more, which I threw out when that got stale. Doris had taken some shriveled carrots, limp celery and cabbage, plus an old chicken she'd found at the back of the freezer and transformed them into a succulent meal. She had also cleaned the kitchen till it shone and totally organized the pantry.

A plate of bacon and eggs appeared under my nose, followed by a stack of pancakes and a cup of coffee. I started eating and Doris started talking.

I learned that she'd been widowed over a year ago, that she and her husband had farmed some acreage up in the northern part of the state, that they had one son who didn't want to be a farmer and had moved to

Hawaii and married, that after her husband's death, she'd sold the farm and moved in with her son, that she couldn't get along with her daughter-in-law, and had packed up her meager belongings to move back to Wadesboro, Indiana, to be with her cousin, her only remaining relative apart from her son. The only thing she didn't talk about was the incident at the airport.

I waited for a break in the torrent of words that washed over me and asked, "Doris, who was that man at the airport?"

There was a moment of complete silence, then, "I already told you, Kate, I don't know—he must have got me mixed up with someone else."

She got up and started fiddling with one of the pots on the stove.

I didn't believe her. When I'd asked the question, her face had blanched and her hands had started to shake. I let it go for now and concentrated on the rare treat of bacon and eggs for breakfast.

Over the next few days, I called her cousin many times, but there was still no answer. Doris seemed in no hurry to leave my home or my company. Despite the fact that she was an eighty-year-old human dynamo who loved cleaning, and cooked just like my grandma used to, after the second week of Doris' society, I wondered if she planned on staying permanently.

My daughter Ellie called. "Mom, how was your vacation?"

What could I say? I'd never intended to go to Hawaii in the first place. Ellie had been hounding me to join her and her family on their annual trek up to Lake Wawasee, in Northern Indiana. I love my daughter though I don't like her too well at the moment, but that's another story, or maybe all part and parcel of the same one. I knew if I spent two weeks in a tiny lakeside cottage with my three-year-old twin grandsons and a disapproving son-in-law, I would feel trapped. Sooner or later Ellie, and her husband Andrew, would dredge up my divorce and want to—as they put it—talk it through. All I wanted was to bury myself in a deep hole and forget the whole thing. I also knew they would be "observing" me for any sign of mental instability and I'd had enough of that in the psych. ward. So when Ellie had brought up the lake cottage vacation for the third time, I'd said, "Oh, the end of July? I forgot to tell you, I already booked a trip."

"To where?"

The only thing that came into my head was a poster I'd seen years ago of blue ocean, palm trees and hula dancers in grass skirts. So I blurted out, "Hawaii." And once I said it, I had to go through with it.

Ellie was waiting for an answer, so instead of talking about my trip, where I seemed to be the only miserable single woman in a crowd of happy couples, I told her about Doris and that she was staying with me for a few days.

"You took in a complete stranger?" I could tell Ellie thought I was still crazy.

"She was stranded at the airport. She's only staying until we contact her cousin."

"I'm coming over right now."

It didn't go well. Ellie sat on the couch glaring at Doris as if she were some interloper, which I guess she was, while I tried to make up a glowing report of my lousy Hawaiian vacation. Doris was no help. She kept up a running litany of everything she'd found wrong with "Hu-why-yuh."

"The beach was gorgeous—miles and miles of golden sand."

"Smelled fishy."

"Wonderful restaurants."

"Nothing but rice and stuff—didn't have one decent meal the whole time I was there."

"The hotel was fantastic."

Doris' loud sniff was her only comment.

Ellie rolled her eyes at me and gave up. As soon as she left, I told Doris that the next morning we would drive up to her cousin's office to find out where he was.

The next day was beautiful, a brilliant blue sky dotted with a few wispy puffs of clouds that floated over the lush green cornfields. The heat and humidity of the past two months were gone, and the roadside ditches were filled with bright orange day lilies intermingled with vivid blue cornflowers and creamy Queen Anne's lace.

I drove with the windows down, enjoying the soft breeze and rich earthy smell of a late summer Indiana day. Doris' cousin lived in the small town of Wadesboro in the northern part of the state.

"I married Otis and we bought a farm over in Pulaski County," she began. "My cousin Charlie was the smart one in the family. He went to Indiana University down in Bloomington and got one of them MBA degrees. He had a good job with an accounting firm in Indianapolis for a few years, but he didn't take to life in a big city. So he moved back to Wadesboro and opened his own office."

She added, "Charlie didn't want me to move to Huh-why-yuh."

She didn't say why and I didn't ask.

"My son, Tommy, went to Indiana University, too. Then he moved to Honolulu for his graduate work."

She was vague about what her son did other than he had an important job with an international company. When I tried to find out why she'd moved back from Hawaii, I got nothing but a stone wall. Doris talked

about the terrible food, the terrible weather—too hot—
but nothing about what had precipitated what seemed to
be a very hurried move—so hurried that she'd called
her cousin to come pick her up the day of the flight.

"I wasn't going to stay there and be treated like
that."

"Like what?" I asked.

The shutters came down and she changed the
subject. "I need to use the bathroom."

This was the third pit-stop. If she didn't buy a cup of
coffee every time we stopped, then gulp it down so she
could have a free refill to take with her, we would have
made much better time. As it was, the two hour drive
turned into three and, as Doris reminded me, it was past
lunchtime when we arrived in Wadesboro.

Her cousin's office was a small, red brick building
on a quiet, tree-shaded street. I parked under a large oak
and left the windows down. As we walked up the path
to the office door, an old black dog on the front yard
across the street barked loudly, and I saw the curtains
twitch.

The door was locked. I knocked and peered through
the window, but all the lights were off and I couldn't
see inside. A woman came out of the house opposite.
She stood on the porch with arms crossed over her
chest, and stared at us. I started to walk over to her, but
she abruptly turned, went back into the house and
slammed the door behind her. Not a friendly place,
Wadesboro.

"Doris, I don't think your cousin's in his office.
Does he live close by?"

"He lives in the apartment upstairs."

She led me down the side of the building next to the
alley. There was a parking pad but no car, and a flight
of wooden steps that led to a small covered porch and a
door. I ran up them and rang the bell. I could hear the

sound echoing in the distance, but the whole place had an empty feel to it and nobody answered.

Doris didn't seem concerned. "Sometimes he has to go down to Indianapolis to meet with clients and such. Or he could be having lunch at the diner. Why don't we check there? It's just around the corner on Main Street."

I left the car where it was and we walked. A lot of people were sitting out on their front porches. They stared as we passed but nobody smiled or nodded.

The diner was the kind found in any small Indiana town—old storefront—screen door that had seen better days, and an air conditioner that wheezed and clanked. We entered, only to garner another round of stares from the people sitting there, and found a table. It was still sticky from the previous occupants. Doris ordered the daily special from the plump and pretty waitress, who was dying of curiosity to find out why two strangers were in town.

"You folks here visiting someone? Or just passing through?"

I answered her by asking for iced tea, and she proceeded to wipe all the loose crumbs off the table into my lap.

"Do you know where we could find...?"

I looked at Doris for her cousin's name.

"Charlie—Charlie Latham."

The waitress stopped in mid-swipe. "Charlie?"

The small knot of men at the next table broke off their conversation and stared at us, mouths hanging open.

"Yes, Charlie Latham. He has the office down the street."

The waitress looked at me and at the next table. She took off for the back of the counter where she whispered in the ear of the other waitress and pointed towards us. The second waitress disappeared through a pair of swinging doors, and the whole diner sat silent, staring at us.

Just as I was about ready to fetch my own tea, the diner door swung open and two uniformed law enforcement officers entered. The older, heavyset man stood by the door surveying the entire room. His eyes landed on Doris and me. The younger policeman walked over to the counter and started an animated conversation with our waitress. I saw her point in our direction. Without waiting for his partner, the first officer made his ponderous way to our table.

Doris and I watched him. The whole diner watched with us.

"You the ladies who were just over at Charlie Latham's office?"

We nodded, yes.

"Would you come with us, please?"

"Why? What's happened?"

The officer didn't answer my question except to say, "We just need a little information, ma'am. It shouldn't take long."

This wasn't parking in the wrong place or violating some small town speed trap; it was something serious. Doris felt it too. Not a word escaped her tightly compressed lips as she gathered up her purse and cardigan. In the waiting police car, she started to shake, and I put my arm around her thin shoulders.

The police station was one town over from Wadesboro. We were shown into a small room and the two officers began to question us.

"You were seen trying to enter Charlie Latham's office. Would you tell us why?"

I looked at Doris. Her voice was shaking and she didn't seem able to answer, so I did it for her. I also had to explain how we met, and where she'd been living for the past two weeks.

"So you didn't know Mrs. Weppler until you sat next to each other on the flight back from San Diego?"

"Correct. Mr. Latham was supposed to pick her up at the airport, but he never turned up, so I took her home with me. We tried calling him and couldn't get an answer. We decided to drive here today to see if we could contact him."

Finally, Doris managed to choke out, "Why are you asking all these questions about Charlie? Has something happened to him?"

The younger, soft-voiced officer put his hand on Doris' arm. "I'm really sorry to have to tell you this, ma'am, but your cousin Charlie is dead. He was shot, murdered, the morning of the day you and your friend flew back from Hawaii."

Doris had been clinging to my hand. There was one gasping intake of breath before she collapsed.

The officer moved quickly. The chair he was sitting on fell over with a resounding crash. He barked out something to whoever was in the corridor outside. Almost immediately a female officer came in with some ice water for Doris. I supported her as she slowly sipped. Then she took a deep breath and sat upright.

The young officer patted her hand. "Are you sure you're up to this? We could do it another day."

Doris shook her head. "Just tell me what happened."

The two officers looked at each other, and the older one nodded. The soft-voiced officer continued, "First, we had no way to contact you. We didn't find them until the next morning. Whoever did it took the telephone and answering machine with them so we never got any messages from you."

"You said them?"

"His secretary was killed too."

The details were sketchy. They were shot, as far as the police could tell, in the late morning. Nobody in Wadesboro had seen or heard anything.

"It was one of the hottest days of the year, ma'am," the younger policeman offered apologetically. "Most everyone was inside, trying to stay cool."

No motive had been discovered. Charlie was well liked. His secretary had worked for him for twenty years. Though there were lots of rumors, nobody could come up with any motive. The general opinion was someone must have had a grudge against Charlie, or else it was an aborted robbery attempt.

"Though it didn't look as if anything was missing, or that the office had been searched. Maybe, ma'am," this to Doris, "when you've had time to think on this more, we can talk again."

I looked at Doris—the gray face and trembling body—she was a frail old woman again. I heard myself say, "Doris, why don't you come back with me until you figure out what you want to do."

And we made the long, but this time silent, trip back to Shelbyville.

Chapter 3

Up until a few months ago I was the perfect wife with a perfect husband and a perfect marriage. Then I got divorced.

I had always been the "good child" in the family, the one who didn't cut class, drink or smoke pot. My older sister did all three before running away to San Francisco with her high school dropout boyfriend and Dad had to fly there to bring her home. But I was the one who studied, did my homework and got good grades—Little Miss Perfect—that was me. So how could I admit to my parents and sister that my idyllic life and marriage had fallen apart? We weren't particularly close. My sister lived in Northern California and my divorced mother and father lived in Boca Raton, Florida, and Scottsdale, Arizona, respectively. Communication between us was sporadic at best.

At first, I didn't tell them about the divorce because I simply didn't have the energy for the explanations they would have wanted. The longer I put off telling them, the harder it became. The previous Christmas, even though the divorce was already filed, I sent cards from "The Conley Family," hoping to delay the inevitable. Since my husband and I were not officially divorced, just in the process, I told myself I hadn't actually lied— I just hadn't told all the truth. But the knowledge that my family would eventually find out hung over me like a black cloud.

I had met Jack my freshman year of college. He was five years older than me, handsome, and to my mind sophisticated. I was homesick and lonely, having just broken up with my high school sweetheart. A few months later, we were married. Over my mother's furious objections, I quit school and worked to put him through law school. It was what you did back then.

When Jack passed the bar, we moved to Shelbyville. It was the county seat of a mainly agricultural area a few miles from Indianapolis, the state capital. Although we didn't meet until college, it was home town for both of us. Jack opened his own law office. I worked as his secretary for the first few years. Then Ellie was born, and the office was successful enough that Jack could afford to hire a secretary, so I stayed home to become a full-time wife and mother.

A few months before the divorce, back when I still thought I had a flawless marriage, Jack came home from the office with a question for me. "How would you like to go to Paris?"

I was stunned. "Paris?"

"A group of my golf buddies are going and taking their wives with them. We could make it the honeymoon we couldn't afford when I was in law school and celebrate our thirtieth wedding anniversary at the same time. What do you say?"

"Yes."

The next day I went shopping for new luggage, made sure our passports were in order and started planning the trip. I had put aside the guide book to Paris and was trying to decide between the Loire Valley chateaux and the wineries of Burgundy when a contrite Jack walked into the kitchen and broke the bad news.

"I'm sorry Kate; I was a little premature. This new client I've taken on is going to take a lot more time than

I realized. What if we go to Paris in the spring, instead?"

Like any dutiful wife, I swallowed my disappointment, hugged him and said, "Paris in the springtime would be even better."

So we marked our thirty-year anniversary with a weekend in southern Indiana on the understanding that the real celebration would be in the spring. We stayed in a historic B&B, the kind I loved, dripping with lace and crystal chandeliers. It may not have been France, but it was a beautiful, romantic weekend. Jack and I walked hand in hand around the picturesque downtown, browsing through antique stores, walking along the banks of the Ohio River before ending up at a quaint little German restaurant. It was heavenly and I could see us growing old together, still walking hand in hand down life's rose-covered path forever.

That was before everything went to hell.

It began with Jack's new secretary, or personal assistant, as she wanted to be called. Mrs. Carter, Jack's longtime secretary, had retired and Tiffany was her replacement. According to Jack, Tiffany learned quickly, was good with clients and, unlike Mrs. Carter, didn't mind working overtime when business warranted. I never saw her as any kind of threat. Sure she was blond, pretty, with an ample figure, but she was only two years older than our daughter and giggled a lot.

The day my life fell apart started out like any other. I was at the country club attending a board meeting for our local museum. We met monthly for lunch and discussion of any issues that arose. The big topic this month was the search for a new director. The discussion went on and on and ended up tabled until the following month, which was typical—we weren't much of a board, but then it wasn't much of a museum.

I had gathered up my belongings, hoping to escape before I was roped in for any new committees, when I saw Bitch Barbara heading towards me.

Bitch Barbara was the wife of Jack's accountant. I met her when Jack and I were first married. She seemed so perfect back then; she intimidated me. She was a wonderful cook, entertained beautifully, sat on just about every committee at church and was so sweet she made my teeth ache.

Early in our marriage, Jack and I had been invited to dinner to meet her brother-in-law and his new wife. The meal was, of course, perfect. The brother-in-law and his wife were great company—sweet, funny and obviously in love. Barbara served coffee and dessert in the living room while Robert, her husband, set up the slide projector. She wanted us to see the pictures of their latest vacation, which seemed a small price to pay for such an excellent dinner.

Then, in the middle of the Grand Canyon, up popped a picture of the beaming brother-in-law with his blushing bride, walking down the aisle together. The problem was it was wife number one, not the current bride. Barbara squealed in horror, put her hand over the projector lens just to make sure nobody missed it and apologized profusely, stating she had no idea how that particular slide could possibly have been mixed up with the vacation ones. But her beady little eyes gleamed and I knew she had done it deliberately, out of sheer spite, to embarrass her new sister-in-law. That's when I named her Bitch Barbara.

Now I saw that same gleam in her eyes as she hurried over to my table, and I wondered whose reputation was up for shredding.

"Kate, darling." She grabbed my hand. "Are you all right? You must be devastated."

The other board members crowded the table like wolves moving in for the kill, and I seemed to be the prey. My confusion must have shown on my face because Bitch Barbara put her hand up to her mouth, no doubt to hide her smirk, and then dropped the little bombshell she had so carefully prepared.

"I'm so sorry. I thought you knew about Jack and Tiffany."

And then I did.

I have no excuse for what happened next except that a few days prior, I was in my little fairy tale—the one that had Jack and me trotting down life's rose-covered path forever. I left the club. I must have driven straight to the office. I just don't remember doing it. I do remember opening the locked outer door with my key and walking into the deserted front office.

Jack's door was ajar. At first, the strange moans and grunts barely registered. Then the pieces coalesced. I moved swiftly to the door to find Jack and Tiffany busily engaged in the act of congress on top of his desk. Some people might argue that *where* Jack committed his adultery had no relevance, but I had bought that desk for his fiftieth birthday. I had spent months scouring antique stores and estate sales to find exactly the right one. He told me he would always cherish it and, at his party, had toasted me as the perfect wife who had found the perfect gift. And here he was screwing his sleazy little secretary—sorry, personal assistant—on its beautifully finished top.

This was Jack's golf afternoon. His clubs were leaning against the wall by the door. I picked out a sturdy one, walked silently over the thick carpet to the desk and brought it down as hard as I could on Jack's wildly heaving buttocks.

He gave an anguished howl, shot up in the air and fell on the floor. He lay there face down and dazed, the perfect target for my next blow. I hit him dead center. He screamed and crawled under the desk to get away. I ran around to the other side, caught him as he scuttled out and got in a few more good licks.

Meanwhile, Tiffany ran shrieking into the outer office and called the police. When they arrived, I was swinging the club over my head, screaming, "You utter bastard," at the top of my lungs, along with a lot of other words I didn't know that I knew. Tiffany was crouched in a corner, crying hysterically. Jack was simultaneously pulling up his pants with one hand and hopping around the office trying to protect his head from the flailing golf club with the other.

He was unsuccessful.

I was handcuffed and taken to our local jail while an ambulance took Jack to the emergency room for treatment of a concussion and bruised ribs.

I got the house, the furniture and half the marital assets. Tiffany got my life and my Paris honeymoon.

Chapter 4

I live in an "emerging" neighborhood in Shelbyville which, in spite of being the county seat, isn't the most exciting city in Indiana. Its main attraction is its proximity to Indianapolis, which is a charming small town big city, if that makes any sense. Shelbyville missed out on the charm factor, lost most of its historic neighborhoods and ended up with a small core of late, 19th century homes surrounded by 1950's brick ranch houses. I chose to live in the historic core, two blocks from the town square.

On my street, beautifully restored homes sit cheek by jowl with total wrecks that have chain link fences and sagging porches. The house I live in was one of the lucky ones. It had been converted into three apartments. The first floor was rented by two women who were artists of some sort. They used the old carriage house on the alley as their studio. I had the second floor, and the third was sublet by a college professor, who was spending her sabbatical in Greece. The new tenant was a sullen young man who wore ripped jeans and stained tee-shirts. He always dropped his eyes and ignored my muttered good mornings whenever we passed on the stairs, which was fine with me.

I had started to volunteer at the old Carnegie library which was two blocks away from the house. Originally, it was a way to fill up my time, but as I got to know the staff and other volunteers, I found myself looking forward to my four-hour stints of re-shelving books. I hoped that nobody knew about Jack and me. The arresting officer had threatened to charge me with aggravated assault, but Jack refused to press charges. My lawyer argued for my impaired mental state and I spent three weeks in an Indianapolis hospital receiving psychiatric treatment. Meanwhile, the divorce was pushed through. Jack tried to hush everything up, but he should have known better. Not much happens in Shelbyville. Someone leaked the story to the press. The headlines blared, *Wife chases cheating husband with his own golf club*. It took a truckload of hogs overturning on I-74, before my page one story was relegated to the back of the newspaper.

My first day at the library, one of the librarians asked me if I was the woman who'd caught her husband tupping his secretary and chased him with a golf club. When I admitted to it, she said, "Way to go. I hope you got the bastard good," and high-fived me. So I stopped worrying about my notoriety.

Doris stayed. We slipped into a comfortable routine. She cooked, cleaned, and generally looked after the house and me. I volunteered at the library and took Doris wherever she wanted to go.

One Sunday morning, we were relaxing over a late breakfast and the newspaper. I looked at the lavish spread set out on the kitchen table—blueberry pancakes, bacon, sausages, creamy scrambled eggs, toast, marmalade and a big pot of tea. There were definite advantages to having a roommate, especially a roommate who loved to cook.

"So when you chased him with the golf club, did you get that little chippie too?"

I choked on my mouthful of pancake, but managed to stop laughing and answer her. "No, I concentrated on Jack."

Doris sniffed. "Pity, anyway he deserved everything he got. I'd have given him a butt load of buckshot—him and his little bimbo." She patted my hand. "No right thinking person would blame you for what you did."

I wasn't sure about that. It still shocked me that I could have been so violent, but in Doris' eyes I could do no wrong. We could be in a store and if she saw a woman dressed in something she deemed inappropriate, she would give one of her sniffs and mutter a judgmental, "Look at that mutton dressed as lamb." I could probably walk around naked and the only thing she'd worry about would be if I were getting chilled.

And she was company. Before she came, I had no social life. I'd shut myself away from my former friends. I didn't want to discuss the divorce with them and I especially didn't want to talk about my stay in the psychiatric ward and Jack's hospitalization.

My daughter Ellie had changed, too. She and her husband Andrew treated me as if I were an unstable explosive, liable to go off at any moment. That I could handle. What I didn't count on was that she and Tiffany would become best friends.

I had driven to her house a few weeks ago on impulse, hoping to close some of the distance between us. I was almost there when I saw Tiffany pulling into the driveway ahead of me. I drove past, parked under a tree on the opposite side of the street, and watched in the rear-view mirror as she walked up to the house and rang the bell. Ellie opened the door. I saw them hug, and Tiffany knelt down and hugged my grandsons, too. They were all laughing. The pain I felt was almost as if a knife had been thrust into my heart and no matter what excuses I made for Ellie, it still felt like a complete and utter betrayal. I pulled into the shopping mall down the street and leaned over the steering wheel until the thudding in my chest slowed down.

The same day, my son-in-law, Andrew, called to ask if I was frivolously wasting the money that would eventually pay for the retirement home they both saw looming in the not so distant future. That may not have been exactly what he said, but that's what I heard. I politely—or maybe not so politely—told him what he could do with his financial advice and that door slammed shut too.

There was Jack tooling around town in his red Porsche, all sun tanned and newly hirsute, with blond and nubile Tiffany by his side, the picture of rejuvenation, while I was being prepared for the old folk's home. Never mind that Jack was a living cliché and looked slightly ridiculous, I was still angry.

That's why I admired Doris. She didn't let life passively pass her by as I was doing. Our downstairs neighbors, Enid and Rose, were now our friends. Doris had started a neighborhood watch group. Mrs. Turner— I had no idea of her first name—was our watch dog and enforcer. She was a shut-in who lived in a neat little cottage across the alley and who spent most of her time looking out of her window anyway. Now she had a legitimate reason. She called the police when necessary, and we could sleep soundly knowing we were in safe hands. In return, Enid cut her grass, Rose helped with the house cleaning she was unable to manage, Doris grocery shopped for her and I, for my part, returned her library books.

Doris also policed the alley behind the house. She complained to the neighbors that she was tired of picking up trash from their garbage cans and they were responsible for keeping their section of the alley clean. Of course, they no longer spoke to us, but the alley looked a lot better. She joined our local community theater, was making a quilt with a group at the Senior Center, and fed the homeless one day a month.

I worked at the library and came home to an immaculate house, with a hot dinner waiting for me.

"What are you going to do with yourself?" she asked me about a month after she moved in.

"I don't know yet."

She was silent for a moment. "It takes time."

I knew she was talking about herself too.

We heard little about the still unsolved murder of her cousin. The police told her they would contact her when the body would be released for burial. And she refused to talk about the man who'd tried to abduct her at the airport. So we went on day by day, and the question of Doris' future remained undiscussed.

Chapter 5

It was a wet and windy Wednesday and I had the morning shift at the library. The last thing Doris said to me as I left the house was, "Take your umbrella. It's going to rain."

Of course, I forgot and arrived at work damp and windblown. Since the library was only two blocks from the house, I rarely drove. It was easier to slip down the back stairs, through the alley, and down the street. The rain started half a block from the building, and I had to sprint the last few yards, arriving out of breath.

"Kate, I need to talk to you."

Sebastian, our library manager, waved me over. He was directing the play at our community theater and wanted me to take a small non-speaking part he'd been unable to cast. But appearing onstage, even in a role that had no lines, was way outside my comfort zone.

I waved back and hurriedly detoured through the Children's Section. I planned on staying out of his way for the rest of the day.

"Hi, Kate, did you have time to do that research I needed?"

Jenna, our children's librarian, stopped me as I tried to breeze past her desk. She was putting together a Civil War program for our local fourth graders. Since she was in the middle of a complete reorganization of the Children's Section, I'd volunteered to do some of the research based on my museum experience.

Still watching for Sebastian, I quickly ran over what I'd found. "I've got some great hardtack recipes we could use. It's basically flour, water, and salt. We'll have the students measure ingredients, then mix and shape the biscuits. They could go outside to practice drills while the biscuits bake in the break-room oven. I'm working on marching formations now and I know a Civil War re-enactor who would love to help."

"Great!" She smiled her thanks and turned back to the impatient children, all wanting to exchange their summer reading points for prizes.

I looked behind me. Sebastian was heading my way. I quickly darted into the stacks and kept out of sight until I reached the break room.

"There you are, Kate."

He caught up to me as I was opening the door. So much for trying to avoid him. Sebastian was a big, round teddy bear of a man, and so adorable almost every volunteer was half in love with him. My feelings were strictly platonic, which was just as well since Sebastian was gay and his partner, Stephen, was my beautician. Dates were hard enough to find, at least that's what I heard from those who were trying, but someone who could cut hair the way you wanted was priceless and no way would I have done anything to upset Stephen.

"Please come to rehearsal tonight. Just give it one try. I promise if you are really uncomfortable, I won't ask you again"

I sighed. I didn't want to go, but Sebastian looked at me with his big, pleading eyes. I couldn't resist.

"I'll probably be terrible, but I'll be there."

He gave me a kiss on the cheek. "I have a feeling you'll be great."

After my shift ended, I took the shortcut home through the alley and came up the back stairs into the kitchen. I heard voices coming from the living room.

"Poor Petey, he was in such pain. How could he kick him like that?"

I hurried into the room to find our downstairs neighbors, Rose and Enid. Rose was clutching a wad of damp tissues in one hand and a cup of herbal tea in the other. She always had an air of fragility about her as if the slightest breeze could waft her away and today she looked as if she should be on a Victorian fainting couch, instead of my comfortable sofa. Her blond, curly hair, which hung halfway down her back, was more disheveled than usual, and the hand holding my best, bone china cup was shaking. Tears welled up in her red-rimmed eyes and spilled down her porcelain face.

"Petey's so traumatized he'll never go outside the door again."

Enid sat next to Rose, rubbing her back. Her short, black hair was standing on end and she was scowling. "If I'd been here that man would be the one traumatized—I'd have kicked *him* down the stairs."

I looked to Doris for clarification.

"Petey was on the stairs today and our upstairs tenant tripped over him and kicked him. He said it was an accident, but I have my doubts—he's a nasty young man. Poor Petey's leg was broke. Rose and I just got back from the vet."

"Here, honey." She took the cup out of Rose's hand and replaced it with a plate of hot buttered scones. "Eat these, you'll feel better. Petey will be fine and we'll pick him up tomorrow."

Coming into the conversation late, I was trying to figure out who Petey was. Then I remembered. He was the black and white cat I occasionally saw on the landing, the one who hissed at me the first and only time I tried to pet him.

"There's something wrong with a person who hates animals. Have you noticed how he skulks around the place?"

Actually, that was Petey, but Rose's pale blue eyes were locked on mine and I could only nod my agreement. I rarely saw the upstairs tenant. Once we almost ran into each other when I rounded a corner of the stairs and he was coming down. I don't know which of us had been the more surprised. He pushed past me and went out the front door, leaving a faint odor of pot in his wake.

"Mrs. Turner says there's all kinds of different people sneaking up the back stairs to his apartment. She's keeping a log like the police told her. She says it looks suspicious."

Doris handed me a cup of tea and a scone and I sat down to hear about the rest of her day.

Chapter 6

I was trying to think of some way to get out of rehearsal that evening but I couldn't come up with anything. Doris had volunteered to help make costumes, Enid was designing the set and also driving us there, so I couldn't use the 'got lost on the way' excuse.

In the car, Enid told me the theater was a converted church and perfect for a theater, having a good-sized stage and a raked floor. I wasn't sure what a *raked* floor was, but she sounded as if it were something everyone should know so I decided not to question it and expose what a rank amateur I was.

When we walked in through the side door from the parking lot, the sheer volume of noise assaulted my ears. A crowd of people were gathered in front of the stage. I didn't recognize any of them. I heard squeals of laughter and disjointed threads of conversation.

"Melia, I haven't seen you since we worked together in *Molly Brown*."

"That was such a great show."

"Have you heard Terry is doing the set for *Into the Woods,* at Buck Creek?"

"Remember when we were both in *Ann Frank,* and his set fell down in the middle of the second act?"

There was more hysterical laughter.

"I hope he's learned how to brace flats."

"I'm dying to find out what Sebastian is going to do to this play. Have you heard anything, Mark?"

Mark had to be the skinny man with the receding chin and fake English accent. "Not yet. Of course, I wouldn't have considered playing such a small role, except that Sebastian begged me to take the part. I was going to audition for Frederic in *Pirates of Penzance,* at Footlite, in Indianapolis."

"Only he doesn't have a hope in hell of being cast, because he can't sing, act, or dance, and he's too old to play Frederic," someone whispered in my ear. I turned to find a little woman standing behind me. She looked like a younger version of Doris except her hair was salt and pepper with a few blond strands threaded through.

"I'm Margaret. I'm doing the costumes for the show. You must be Kate, Doris' roommate."

Technically, Doris was *my* roommate, but I let it go and quickly introduced myself.

"So you're the one who's playing the maid. Wait till you see the costume we designed for you, you'll love it."

I was sure I wouldn't. I felt certain I couldn't fulfill the extremely high expectations Sebastian seemed to have of me. The only time I'd ever been onstage was at my high school graduation. Even then I tripped as I went down the steps after collecting my diploma.

I seemed to be the only novice there. I wondered if I could slip out while everyone was catching up with each other but I left it too late. Doris reappeared, grabbed my arm, waded right in and towed me behind her. Being Doris, she knew everyone, introduced me so many times my head started to spin. "This is Kate. It's her first time here and she's going to be our maid."

Sylvia, the librarian who had high-fived me my first day at the library, was playing the lead. Frank, another of our library volunteers, was helping Enid build the set. I'd already met Margaret. My beautician, Stephen, was going to do hair and makeup. There was a stage manager, people for props, lighting, sound—and they would all see me make a complete fool of myself.

"Places everyone!"

Immediately, the chatter stopped. I was handed a script even though I had no dialogue, and given my mark onstage.

"We'll take it from the top of the dinner scene. Kate darling," Sebastian was suddenly more theatrical now that he was away from the library—he was tossing the "darlings" around like candy. "What I want you to do in this scene is put the plates in front of everyone, starting with Mark."

That seemed simple enough. I already knew who Mark was. Unfortunately, the scene was a lot more complicated. I had to place the plates in front of the actors on specific lines of dialogue, and I was terrified of getting it wrong. The more the scene progressed, the more nervous I became. By the time I got to the head of the table where I was supposed to serve the matriarch of the family played by Sylvia, my hands were shaking and the plate slipped and landed with a resounding crash. Sylvia gave a startled squeak and everybody laughed.

"Wonderful, darling. Let's leave that in."

We did it again, and this time Sebastian told me to put the plate down harder. Sylvia almost shrieked and everyone laughed again. All the actors reacted to the bit of business and I felt as if a star were born.

"Do you think you could make the maid a little more slutty?"

Of course, I could do slutty. I had only to think of Tiffany with her low cut tops and silly giggle.

"Could you make some kind of bitchy gesture as you pass Sylvia?"

I rolled my eyes, looked at the audience, pointed, and mouthed, "Silly cow."

Sylvia moaned and clutched her throat. Everyone fell about laughing again.

We worked on the scene a few more times before moving on. While the rest of the cast rehearsed, I sat in the auditorium with my script, carefully highlighting every scene in which the maid appeared. I hadn't read the play. I didn't know the title. But I was totally hooked on theater.

Later, at the Pancake House, the only place open at that time of night, Sylvia told me the play was a total dog, written by the late founder of the group and trotted out as a fund raiser every few years. This year, Sebastian had drawn the short straw and since he was not allowed to change any of the dialogue, had the brilliant idea to make it a comic farce, instead of the plodding, overwrought melodrama originally conceived. He had decided to use the maid as the main comic relief.

Frank told me I had a natural gift for comedy. Sylvia had suggestions for new bits of business. Margaret and Stephen had ideas for hair and costumes. The only person who didn't seem happy was Mark. I heard him tell Sebastian, "I don't know why the maid has to be funny. Nobody's ever done it that way before."

I floated home on—as Doris would say—cloud nine.

I should have remembered that she also said, "Pride goeth before a fall."

Chapter 7

It really was a dark and stormy night. Lowering skies with thunder rumbling in the distance, almost tornado weather, except it was a little late in the year for tornados. I would have liked to have stayed home curled up on the sofa with a glass of wine and a good book. Instead, Doris and I were invited to Rose's art exhibit in Fountain Square, on the south side of Indianapolis. This was another "emerging" neighborhood and the art gallery was a converted, 19th century warehouse.

Rose's work was not what I expected. I had figured her for delicate flower paintings. Instead her canvases were large and bold, almost primal, loaded with heavy swirls of vitriolic paint. Standing in front of them, I felt as if I were being drawn into some place dark and menacing. I decided to calm my nerves with a glass of wine so I headed for the bar.

I lost Doris to the free appetizers, but she emerged later, art patrons hanging on her every word, as she interpreted the paintings for them. "This is from her blue period when everything in her life was sheer chaos, and this is reflected in her *oeuvre* from that time."

She pronounced it "owvura," but it was still impressive.

She gestured wildly at another picture. "And this reflects her life from after she met Enid. You can see the maturity of her line, and the more vibrant palette."

Was she making this up as she went along or had I misjudged her? I was continually underestimating Doris. I had pictured her as a farm wife, whose only interests were cooking, cleaning, and maybe this year's crop prices or hog futures, but here she was flitting around an art gallery, perfectly comfortable with the multi-colored hair, body-pierced and tattooed ambiguous-gender crowd.

I decided to have another glass of the cheap wine and go with the flow. It seemed to be a successful evening. There were a lot of sold tags on the canvases, and the warehouse was crowded.

"Hey, Kate." Frank grabbed my arm and yelled into my ear, to be heard over the din. "After this is over, we're meeting up at Santorini's, the Greek restaurant down the street. See you there. I'll get the table."

He was such a great guy. He'd lost his wife a little over a year ago, after devotedly nursing her through a long illness. Like me, Frank had volunteered at the library to fill the empty hours. Again, like me, he had been roped into helping at the theater and his handyman talents had made him an integral part of the group.

Our librarian, Sylvia, appeared at my shoulder. "See that guy over there—he's my date. I met him online."

I glanced across the room at the portly, middle-aged man anxiously scanning the crowd.

"He looks a little lost."

"Well, I haven't introduced myself yet. I want to check him out first—if he's a dud I'll let him think he's been stood up."

Sylvia found a lot of dates online and according to her, there were many frogs and few princes.

"Won't he recognize you from your picture?"

"Kate, you never put your real picture online—just something close. Tonight I'm an older Brigitte Bardot."

Sylvia did look a little like Bardot. Her wild curly hair was more gray than blond, but she had the pout and sexy eyes.

She giggled, "Time to talk to my anxious swain, to see if he's my prince." And off she danced, wine glass in hand, to meet—as she put it—her destiny. Soon she was back. "Too needy—recently divorced." And she was off again on another hunting expedition.

"Do you see how I'm talking up Rose's pictures? I think I've got three of 'em sold." Doris was ecstatic.

"How do you know so much about art?"

"I don't. Rose lent me a book, but it took too much reading. So I looked at what was printed under all the pictures, and I'm kinda making it up. But those people don't know that and it sounds good, right? Ooh, there's some more."

And off she went to trap other unsuspecting patrons before I could tell her how impressed I was with her fictitious art expertise.

Drinking doesn't really agree with me. I usually pay for it with a thumping headache and tonight was no exception so I was glad when everyone was ready to leave. Enid and Rose would join us later at the restaurant.

At the restaurant, the food was good but the dining room was full of noisy people. The shrieks of laughter bouncing off the walls made my headache worse. I wanted to go home, but Doris was holding court, buzzed on free wine and her success at selling paintings.

"I think I got eight of 'em sold. I bet if we'd stayed longer I could've gotten rid of every last one."

She was good for another couple of hours and I didn't want to burst her bubble. I found Frank. "I've got a headache. I'm going to leave, but Doris…"

"Don't worry, Kate. I'll make sure Doris gets home safe. We're going to stay until Enid and Rose get here, then we'll be right behind you."

Traffic was light. I cut across the parkway to Prospect and up Southeastern over to I-74, rather than pick up the interstate. It took a lot longer, but it was somehow soothing to drive through winding streets and see the old houses that had stood in the same place for over a hundred years. It was—I tried to find the right word—continuity. The houses had sheltered families in good times and bad, and in spite of neglect and poverty, the people and the houses had survived. Wasn't there a lesson there somewhere? Maybe, but I couldn't figure out what it was. I decided I was getting maudlin, another byproduct of the bad wine.

Thunder still rumbled as I parked in the alley. The light outside the entrance to the back stairs had burned out again. This made the third time in two weeks. The back yard was very dark. I briefly considered walking around the side of the house where we had motion lights, and entering through the front door. Then I heard the patter of raindrops on the roof of the car and decided to run for it.

I made my way up the back stairs. The light outside my door was out and I had to fumble in the dark for the lock. My keys were in my hand, but I didn't need them because the door swung open as soon as I touched it. Later, I was asked why I'd entered the apartment when something was so obviously wrong. Why didn't I go back down the stairs and call the police?

I had no answer, except the apartment was my safe place, my sanctuary, though I have no doubt the headache and wine helped. The kitchen lights were off, which I remember thinking odd. We always left at least one burning. I moved cautiously forward, using my feet to feel ahead. The light switch was just past the pantry on the right. Before I got to it, I tripped over something and dropped my keys. I fell forward onto my knees, and put out my hands to save myself. They landed in something wet and sticky. Beyond that was a still, yielding mass.

I forgot the keys and lunged for the light switch. The bright light momentarily blinded me. I frantically blinked until everything came into focus. My hands and the front of my dress were covered in something dark and sticky. I stood there helplessly and stared down at the broken, majolica urn over which I'd tripped. What was it doing in the kitchen? It usually stood by the side of the front door. It was then that I saw the body wedged under the table. I should have left right away and called the police, but my feet seemed to move forward of their own volition. The body was my ex-husband Jack. He was lying on his side with a dark halo surrounding his head and he wasn't moving. How could Jack be in my apartment? I backed away towards the door. I wanted to get out and down the stairs, but I was too terrified to go into the blackness below. So I stood in the little pool of light spilling out from the kitchen and started screaming. I didn't stop until the police came.

I heard the ambulance heading down the street to the hospital. The blaring siren slowly faded in the distance. That was a good thing, I told myself. It meant Jack was still alive. I was in the den, covered in his blood, sitting on the edge of the sofa that served as Doris' bed. I needed a hot shower, anything to get rid of the crawling sensation on my skin, but the police said I had to talk with the detective before I could get cleaned up. A female officer came into the room and put a blanket around my shoulders but it didn't stop the shaking.

It was as if I were at the bottom of a deep well. Everything was happening at a distance. I heard people moving around, but the activity seemed far removed from me. My son-in-law, Andrew, put his head around the door, looked at me and withdrew without speaking.

There were voices in the hallway. I thought I heard Andrew say, "Are you arresting her tonight?" A deeper voice replied but it was muffled, so I didn't hear the answer. I vaguely wondered who they were talking about, but I was too exhausted to care.

The policewoman came back with a cup of hot tea. My hand shook and she put it down on a side table. I pulled myself together enough to thank her, and lapsed back into my fugue state.

Two men came into the room. The one about my age looked familiar. I thought I recognized the piercing, blue eyes and the almost military-looking, gray hair.

He stood over me. "Can you tell me again how you found your husband?"

"Ex-husband, we're divorced."

Then I remembered him. He was the detective who'd handcuffed me and hauled me off to jail after I'd caught Tiffany and Jack together in the office.

The cold blue eyes flickered over me. "You say you left your friends and came home early. Why?"

"Because," I hesitated. I hadn't been drunk but over the course of the evening I'd had three glasses of the atrocious wine, which was two more than I normally drank. And which contributed to the headache, which was the reason I'd left early. He noticed the hesitation and his eyes narrowed.

"I had a headache," I finished lamely.

"Are you sure it wasn't because you'd arranged to meet your ex-husband at your apartment?"

"No. Why would I? Jack has never been here. I didn't think he even knew where I lived. We've had no contact since the divorce."

"Then how do you explain his ending up on your kitchen floor in a pool of blood?"

I shook my head. "I can't."

There was a commotion in the hallway. Doris, Rose and Enid pushed their way into the room.

"Sorry, sir, couldn't stop them," the young police officer muttered.

Rose put her arms around me and I clung to her.

Doris waved her finger under the detective's nose, which she could barely reach. "You leave her alone. Can't you see she's in shock? Her lawyer is on the way, and he says you're not to talk to her without his being here."

Enid and Rose drew me to my feet. "She's coming down to our apartment. You can question her in the morning."

The two detectives took a step towards us. For a moment I thought there would be an old fashioned standoff between Doris, Enid, Rose and the three police officers, with me in the middle.

The older detective relaxed. He nodded to the policewoman. "Go with them."

The policewoman waited until I undressed, then took my clothes away with her. I stood under a scalding shower until the water ran cold, trying to get rid of any trace of Jack's blood. Enid gave me a t-shirt to sleep in and Rose made up a bed for me on the couch. The last thing I remembered was Petey butting his head up under my chin, and snuggling his warm little body next to mine. I fell asleep to his soft purring.

Chapter 8

And so began what I thought of later as the three circles of hell. Doris and I were not allowed back into the apartment for four days. That wasn't hellish, just inconvenient. Doris did manage to get in somehow because the next morning she disappeared and arrived back at Enid and Rose's apartment dragging two suitcases filled with clothes and toiletries, and complaining about the mess the police had left.

"You wouldn't believe how they went through everything. It's going to take me days to get it straight again."

That solved the problem of what to wear when the police car arrived to pick me up and take me in for questioning, which was definitely the first circle of my hell.

"You don't have to say anything until your lawyer gets there," Doris cautioned me.

"Who's my lawyer?"

"You don't have one. I just said that last night so those policemen would leave you alone, but you're supposed to ask for one."

Doris watched a lot of television crime shows.

As I was escorted out, she yelled after me, "Remember the lawyer."

It turned out I didn't need a lawyer because I wasn't charged with anything.

"Your friends say you left the restaurant at approximately eleven-fifteen." That was Detective Williamson, the gray-haired officer with the flinty blue eyes, who told me when he introduced himself that his first name was Sam.

I nodded.

"Please answer the question."

"Yes."

We were sitting almost knee to knee, in a dingy, claustrophobic room at the police station. The whole place smelled vaguely unpleasant, though I couldn't identify the odor—just that it was stale and nasty. The questions centered round why Jack was in my apartment—something I couldn't answer—though it was asked many times, in many ways. The other question repeatedly asked, was what time I arrived home.

"It's a forty minute drive back to Shelbyville from Fountain Square, but the first call about a woman screaming didn't come in to the switchboard until twelve-forty three. That's almost an hour and a half after you left the restaurant."

I nodded again. The young policeman opened his mouth and I quickly answered in the affirmative.

"That's approximately forty-eight minutes unaccounted for."

I took his word for it. I was in no shape to do the math.

"Are you sure you and your husband—ex-husband," he corrected himself before I could, "didn't arrange to meet at your place and maybe things got a little heated. He might have been threatening you and you picked up the closest thing to hand and hit him?"

Jack threatening me? One time at our local market, I almost ran into him. When he saw me walking down the aisle, he turned and headed for the exit. I didn't think it would be smart to volunteer that Jack was too scared to come within a half mile of me.

"No, I told you the light was off. It was dark and I tripped. Jack was on the floor. Then I screamed."

"So what were you doing during those forty-eight minutes?"

I tried to explain about driving through the neighborhoods and looking at the houses, but he interrupted.

"You're saying that instead of an easy drive home on the freeway, which wouldn't be busy at that time of night, you took the long way through some very marginal areas?"

"Yes."

"In spite of a headache severe enough for you to leave a party early?"

"Yes."

He leaned back in his chair and tossed his pen on top of his notebook. "I find that hard to believe."

"Aren't there street cameras or something you could check?"

Doris wasn't the only one who watched police shows, though I didn't believe in them as implicitly as she did.

He ignored the question. "Your husband was hit on the back of the head. It's not as if you haven't done that before, right?"

I knew that would rear its ugly head. "That was months ago and the golf club wasn't that heavy. I did have provocation." I looked at the female officer standing by the door. "How would you feel if you walked in on your husband of thirty years, boffing his personal assistant on top of the antique desk you bought him for his fiftieth birthday?"

She shrugged. "I got rid of mine the second time I caught him with my sister."

Detective Williamson shot her a killer look. The one he gave me wasn't any better. "It sounds as if you're still angry about that."

It was no use. He'd already decided I'd tried to kill Jack, and nothing I could say would change his mind.

Then it was the younger detective's turn. He wanted to know how Jack had entered the apartment. "Neither the front or back door had been forced, so if you locked the doors when you left, as you said, your ex-husband must have had a key."

"No, he didn't."

"Does your daughter have a key? Would she have given him a copy?"

"No and no. The only people with keys are my roommate and myself."

It was as if I were talking to the wind. They asked the same questions over and over. I gave the same answers as before. Detective Williamson took careful note in his small notebook. Just when I thought we'd moved on, they would come back to why I'd left the restaurant before everybody else, the length of time it took for me to drive home, and if Jack didn't have a key to the apartment, someone had to let him in, and the logical conclusion was that that someone had to be me.

Finally, I'd had enough. I was tired of Detective Williamson leaning across the narrow table shooting rapid fire questions at me while his ice-cold, blue eyes bored into mine like a laser. If he was trying for intimidation, it wasn't working. I was just getting angry.

"Either arrest me or let me out of here." I'd heard that many times on *CSI*. I didn't think it would work, but it did. Doris would be disappointed I wasn't told not to leave town, but they did say they would need to question me further.

I didn't realize that meant daily for the next week and a half. The worst part was, though they expected me to answer all their questions over and over again, they would never answer any of mine.

Then it abruptly stopped. At first I thought it was some new tactic designed to squeeze a confession out of me, but after a couple of weeks went by with no phone calls asking me to stop by the precinct, and no knocks at the front door, I decided they were done with me.

Circle two was worse. I went straight from the first day's interrogation to the hospital. Jack was in ICU. Nobody would give me any information on his condition because, though we'd been married for thirty years, that information was only to be given to the spouse or a family member and I no longer qualified.

So I went to the ICU waiting room, not only to find out about Jack, but because I thought Ellie might need me. She and Tiffany were sitting together, and, of course, Tiffany fell into a hysterical fit at the sight of me. Ellie held her and tried to comfort her. She looked at me with accusing eyes. "Just go, Mom." The on-duty nurse called security. I was escorted out and told not to come back.

And I realized my daughter was convinced I was the one who'd attacked her father.

Until I returned to the library, I didn't realize how nervous I was. How would people react to me? The first person I saw was Jenna, the children's librarian. She saw me then quickly turned away and busied herself with a pile of books on the back counter.

I wasn't going to let her ignore me. Moving directly in front of her, I said, "Jenna, I brought all the information you needed for the Civil War program. I thought we could work on it this afternoon."

She swallowed nervously. "I wouldn't have time today."

"Tomorrow then?"

She hesitated, "I'm not sure about tomorrow."

"I can make it any day this week. What's best for you?"

"Kate, maybe we should wait until all this is over."

"All what?"

"This business with your husband."

"Ex-husband," I spat out through clenched teeth.

"It's just the children..." she twittered nervously.

I had done hours of research for the Civil War program we were putting together. The folder I had compiled on the local regiments, the hard tack recipes, marching formations, and the graves and monuments of Shelby County soldiers was thick, but somehow I ripped it in two pieces and tossed them on her desk. Childish but satisfying!

Until I'd attacked Jack with his golf club, I had done everything right. I had been nurturing and supportive. I had gone to all of Ellie's school functions, entertained Jack's friends and business acquaintances, joined the right groups like the museum board, and done everything I could to be the perfect wife and mother.

And I was nice, the most boring word in the English language. I was kind to animals and people. I volunteered at our local museum, donated to various charities, worked once a month at a homeless shelter in Indianapolis, and was a classroom aide at my grandson's pre-school. Of course, after my little *contretemps* with Jack, I was politely told my services were no longer needed at the pre-school, nor at the museum, nor on the museum board for that matter.

I don't think the homeless shelter would have cared, but I quit anyway, and upped my donation to compensate.

Once, in an antique, vintage type store, I saw an embroidered sampler with the message, "Release Your Inner Bitch." At the time, I didn't understand what it meant. Now I completely got it and that's exactly what I was going to do. I was tired of being nice, and sweet, and compliant. What did that get me? A cheating husband, a failed marriage, and a serpent's tooth of a daughter who believed I had plotted to kill her father. It was time to let the bitch out.

I stomped off to find Sebastian. I was ready to tell him what he could do with his volunteer position and his acting gig. He was standing near the librarian's desk talking to Sylvia. I marched up, put my hands on my hips, words ready to tumble out of my mouth, when he saw me.

"Kate, are you all right?" He enveloped me in one of his big bear hugs.

Sylvia came around the desk and hugged me too. "We've all been so worried about you. How are you holding up? Do the police have any idea who attacked your ex-husband?"

Frank came up. He didn't hug me. Frank wasn't a hugger, but he did pat my shoulder, and say it was good to see me back and I'd been missed.

Even bossy Clarice, the volunteer who was the least friendly, wheeled over the carts of fiction she had alphabetized, and told me to hang in there and that things would get better. Since the only time Clarice ever spoke to me was to point out mistakes I made when shelving books, I was dumbfounded.

And right then, the sun did come out, shining through the tops of the leaded glass windows behind the check-out counter. It was as if my winter changed into summer and the whole world was blooming.

"Don't forget rehearsal tonight," were Sebastian's parting words. When I arrived home, I found we had been allowed back into the apartment. Doris had finished cleaning and was cooking a special dinner to celebrate being home again.

"That detective gave me the business card of a place that cleans up crime scenes. As if I needed it. 'Who do you think cleaned up after we slaughtered the hogs?' I asked him. A little bit of blood don't bother me."

Everything was gleaming. The yellow crime tape was gone. Enid had replaced the light bulbs on the back stairs. Rose opened the bottle of wine they had brought up, and even though we ate in the kitchen at the table that had sheltered Jack's unconscious body, we had a great dinner, followed by an even greater rehearsal.

Chapter 9

The fog I was operating in had gone away, but not the anger. I had finally let the bitch out, and she wasn't going back in until I got some answers.

First, what was Jack doing in my apartment? Apart from random incidents when we accidentally almost ran into each other, we had absolutely no contact. In fact, we never met, because if he saw me he immediately ran the other way. I felt a smug sort of satisfaction that I'd scared him enough that he wouldn't risk any kind of confrontation. At some point I might even have fun with it but not yet.

Second, why had the police stopped questioning me? Did they have another suspect? Had Jack recovered enough that he was able to tell them what really happened? I was angry that they could make my life such hell then have it stop, without telling me why.

I decided to tackle Jack first. When I got to the hospital, visiting hours were just starting. Jack was out of ICU and in a private room. Luckily, none of the nurses on the floor recognized me and I was able to breeze into his room unchallenged.

He was reading. When he heard me enter, he looked up and total panic swept across his face.

"Kate, what are you doing here?" His hand went to the call button.

I moved it out of reach. "Don't worry, Jack, you don't need security. I'm not staying long."

His book slid off the bed onto the floor. He made as if to grab it, but it landed with a thud and I kicked it across the room where it hit the wall and skittered under the bed. He watched me warily, his eyes flicking to the call button which I still held in my hand.

"I want to know what you were doing in my apartment."

He looked away. I knew he was going to lie before the words came out of his mouth. "I don't remember. That night is gone—it's the head injury."

"Bullshit, you had a reason for going there and I want to know what it was."

Jack's eyes opened wide. He'd never heard me cuss before. He eyed the door but no help arrived. I kept talking.

"There's no way you accidentally turned up. You went there for something. I'm not leaving until you tell me what it was."

"Kate, I'm very sick. I almost died. I truly can't remember." He leaned back against the pillows and closed his eyes. The bastard was playing the sympathy card.

"How did you get in? I know we locked the doors before we left, which means you must have a key."

"I told you I can't remember. If you don't go, I'm going to call security."

I dangled the call button in front of his face. "With what?"

Leaning in close, I put my mouth against his ear, "I'm not buying that amnesia crap. I know you're lying, and unless you tell me the truth, I'm going to rip your heart out."

I was angry enough to do it but then I heard, "Mom, what are you doing here?"

And there was my loving daughter with best friend Tiffany, standing there aghast with her mouth dropping open.

I smiled sweetly. "Just visiting your father. I was worried about him, and I'm curious as to what he was doing in my apartment."

I took a shot. "I don't suppose you know, do you, Tiffany?"

I got a hit.

"No, I have no idea."

But she was lying too.

Chapter 10

My visit to Jack wasn't exactly fruitful, except I learned that both Jack and Tiffany had lied to me. What I needed to know was why. Maybe I would have better luck at the Shelbyville Police Department? I wanted to find out why the police had stopped questioning me and if they had any other suspects. The officer on the front desk told me Detective Williamson wasn't available.

"Does that mean he's not here or he's too busy to see me?"

"It means he's in a meeting and can't be disturbed."

"Then I'll wait until he's done."

"Suit yourself, ma'am. But he'll be tied up for the rest of the day."

So I suited myself. I sat in plain view of the desk, tapping my foot against the chair. That got no response so I got out my cell phone and started to catch up on calls.

"Sebastian, I'm going to be a couple of hours late to the library today. I'm at the police department and it may take some time."

Of course, Sebastian wanted to know why I was there, so I told him.

The officer moved a sign that said cell phones were to be switched off, to a more prominent place on the counter. I stared him in the eye, shrugged my shoulders, and made another call.

"Sylvia, how was your date last night?"

Of course, it was her usual catastrophe. I settled in for a loud and lengthy conversation.

"You mean you'd dated this guy before until you found out he was married?"

I listened some more. "And he was using a different name and profile? Was he surprised to see you?"

"You mean you were using a different name and profile too?"

Then we both erupted into helpless giggles.

The officer sighed and picked up the phone. Two minutes later, a police officer appeared and escorted me back to one of the interview rooms.

After a brief wait, Detective Williamson walked through the door. He looked irritated.

"I'm sorry I only have a few minutes. What can I help you with?"

"I want to know why the daily interrogations have stopped."

The detective stared at me. Finally, he said, "We're looking in a different direction."

"And what exactly does that mean? Am I no longer a suspect? Do you know who attacked my ex-husband and why it took place in my apartment?"

He refused to meet my eyes. He just sat there like an idiot, twirling his pen in his fingers.

Then reluctantly he said, "We checked the traffic cams. You did take the long way home."

I almost said, *told you so*, but politely refrained.

"And one of your neighbors alibied you."

He paged through his notebook and read out a name. "Mrs. Turner. She's a neighborhood watch coordinator. She called in as soon as you parked in the alley."

"So you know what time I got home?"

"Yes, we do. I'm sorry we missed it." The tips of his ears turned slightly red. "Mrs. Turner is very conscientious. She calls in as soon as someone parks, or walks through the alley. The dispatcher didn't take it seriously and the information wasn't passed along. In their defense, she calls in five or six times a night, but when we checked her log she had you arriving a minute or two before all the calls came in about a woman screaming."

"So you know I didn't plot to kill my ex-husband?"

"We know from the forensic evidence that he had been lying on that floor for close to an hour, so no, you couldn't have been the person who attacked him. It still doesn't explain why he was in your apartment."

"I'd like to know that, too."

He checked his cell phone. "Look, I really have to go but I still have some questions. I'll be out of town all day. Do you have some time this evening?"

I nodded.

"I'll call you when I'm driving back. Maybe we could meet up somewhere, and I'll fill you in on what I can."

"Sure"

And so began the third circle of hell.

Chapter 11

The evening started out fine. I got the call from Detective Williamson as promised. He suggested we meet at Luigi's, a local restaurant, which happened to be a favorite of mine.

He was eating when I arrived.

"I hope you don't mind—haven't had time for anything today."

I didn't mind; this was a business meeting not a social occasion. He looked tired and rumpled, not at all like the squared away police officer I usually saw.

Doris had already fed me so I ordered a glass of wine and waited.

"As I told you this morning, you are no longer considered a suspect in the attack on your ex-husband, but we wondered if you could shed any light on why he was in your apartment?"

"I don't know. I went to the hospital today to ask him that same question."

"And?"

"He said he had amnesia and couldn't remember anything about that night."

He looked at me.

"I didn't believe him either. I saw Tiffany at the hospital and asked her if she had any idea why Jack was in my apartment. She said no, but I'm pretty sure she was lying too."

He grabbed the last piece of bread in the basket, wiped it around his almost empty plate, popped it in his mouth and sat back, pushing his plate to one side. The waiter hurried over with another glass of wine.

He changed the subject. "How long have you known Doris Weppler?"

"About two months. Why do you want to know?"

"She's quite a character. I was wondering how you met."

By now I was on my second glass of wine so I told him about meeting Doris on the plane back from Hawaii, which led to why I went to Hawaii in the first place, which led to the divorce, which led to finding Jack and Tiffany having sex in the office, which led to the romantic thirtieth wedding anniversary, which was the reason I'd lost it and put Jack in the hospital.

"You're quite a hero to a lot of the female officers— not that I'm advocating domestic violence," he added hastily, "but it's something of a joke down at the precinct. The women are calling it—'doing a Conley.' How did you end up with Doris living with you?"

I told him about Doris' cousin not turning up at the airport, and how some man had tried to pull her into his car, and how Doris said it must have been a case of mistaken identity, and how, when I took her up to Wadesboro, her cousin had been murdered and I had no choice but to bring her back to Shelbyville with me.

I paused. I had done most of the talking. Maybe this was part of training to be a detective—you ask the right questions and sit quietly while the subject rattles on about everything under the sun. I noticed how he led the conversation back to the topics he wanted to hear.

The waiter brought a bottle of wine over to the table. He refilled my glass and Detective Williamson's too.

After that, things seemed to get a little fuzzy. Detective Williamson had somehow become Sam and told me he was divorced also. But that was the only personal information he shared.

I seemed to have told him everything about my life, from when I'd first met Jack, to how Ellie believed I was responsible for the attack in my apartment.

"Well, you did put him in the hospital when you attacked him with his golf club."

"But it was just that one time. I haven't been near him since, except for my hospital visit today."

Where I'd terrorized a sick man and lied to my daughter, I thought guiltily.

I did learn something from Sam. Mrs. Turner had reported two people coming out of the house about an hour before I got home. She also reported various comings and goings in the previous weeks, and the fact that someone kept unscrewing the light bulb over the back door, which made identification difficult.

Sam leaned back in his chair. "Look, it's been a rough day. Let's relax over another glass of wine and talk about anything other than the case. You know what I do—tell me how life is treating you these days."

He looked exhausted so I told him about my role as the slutty maid and how at first I hated the idea of appearing onstage but now loved it. His blue eyes crinkled with amusement as I related the ups and downs of rehearsing, the outrageous costume Margaret had designed for me, and the hairstyle Stephen wanted me to wear.

"I love playing the part. I think of my ex-husband's new wife and it's easy."

Sam threw his head back and laughed. He had a great laugh, deep and rich. He was also—I noticed—a rather handsome man with his vivid blue eyes and silver hair.

The first bottle of wine went down so well, we ordered a second. The more we drank, the better looking Sam became and the harder he laughed at my theater stories. By the time the bottle was empty we were a little too tipsy to drive home.

In the parking lot, I decided I was having so much fun I didn't want the evening to end.

"I think we both need coffee."

"Sorry, Kate, there's no place open at this time of night."

"You can't think of any place to go?"

He laughed. "Only coffee I know of right now is in my apartment."

"Let's go. Where do you live?"

Sam looked surprised, but I didn't give him a chance to back out. His apartment was conveniently around the corner. We left the cars at Luigi's and walked the half block. By then I'd decided I no longer wanted coffee. We had another glass of wine instead. You can guess the rest. I don't know if the earth moved exactly, but I think there were a few interesting tremors along the way.

I carefully opened my eyes against the harsh morning light. The sun had crept around the edge of the blind, making a rainbow on the wall as it shone through the empty wine glass on the dresser. My head was pounding. For a moment I was disoriented. I looked over to my right. Next to me in the bed was a gently snoring, Detective Sam Williamson. It hadn't been a bad dream.

I had to get out of there before he woke up. I held my breath and carefully rolled off the bed. My foot hit the bedside table and I froze momentarily, but he didn't move and I was able to grab my clothes and slide out of the room without waking him.

How could I have done it? My recollections were a little hazy but I remembered the restaurant and how easy it was to talk to Sam. I remembered how much I enjoyed laughing over a few glasses of wine with a handsome man who thought my theater stories funny. I remembered how we decided we were too tipsy to drive home. And I remembered that going to Sam's apartment was my idea. Sam was going to call a cab for me.

I needed to get to my car before anyone noticed it had been parked next to his on Luigi's lot all night. I caught a few strange looks as I walked along the sidewalk. Once I was in the car, I checked myself in the rear-view mirror. My mascara had run and I looked like a dissolute raccoon. I grabbed a half empty bottle of water and some tissues from the console and scrubbed my face. It didn't help—I might as well draw a big letter *A* in the center of my forehead, except were you an adulterer if you were already divorced?

I parked as quietly as I could in the alley, crept up the backstairs and through the door into the kitchen, knowing all the while that Mrs. Turner would log my return into her notebook and very likely pass the information on to the police department. Doris was sitting at the table—I was busted. She looked at me, sniffed once and said, "I'll put the kettle on for tea—you're probably not ready for breakfast yet."

The phone rang.

"I'm not here, okay?"

And I wasn't there for the rest of that day, or any of the others, until Sam finally quit calling.

Chapter 12

My hell slowly receded. To her credit, Doris asked no questions about my night with Sam and I decided to get my life in order. First, I was never, ever, going to drink wine again, and I was never, ever, going within three miles of the Shelbyville Police Department or Detective Sam Williamson.

Sam didn't call again but I saw him a week later lurking in the mystery section at the library. I avoided him by ducking into the staff break room and asking Frank to tell me when he left. It was just that one time and that seemed to be the end of it.

A few days later, I arrived home after my afternoon shift at the library to find Doris sitting on the couch staring into space. She looked up when she heard me enter. Her eyes were red and swollen. I sat down next to her and took her hand. "What's wrong?"

She took a shuddering breath and pulled herself together. "It's Charlie. The Wadesboro police called. They're releasing the body and I can bury him now."

Deep sobs racked her tiny frame. I held her until the storm passed, then she pulled away from me. "I'm all right, Kate." She sat upright, blew her nose on a piece of paper towel that she'd taken from the pocket of her apron. "Now I've got to give him a good send-off."

After that, she refused to talk about it again except to give me the date of the funeral.

It was an unseasonably chilly day. The leaves were starting to change color. A strong wind blew them from the trees in great whirling gusts onto the mourners gathered below.

Charlie was buried in the graveyard of the local Methodist Church. He wasn't a churchgoer, but Doris wanted him to stay in the town where he'd grown up. His secretary had been buried the previous week and her family was at Charlie's funeral also. Two funerals in as many weeks—the sadness was reflected in the faces of the townspeople clustered around the grave.

Rose, Enid, Sebastian, Sylvia and all our library and theater friends were there, too. Even Stephen had managed to take a day off from the beauty shop to show his support.

Doris was her usual stoic self, but as she stepped forward to throw a handful of dirt on Charlie's coffin, she wavered and grabbed my arm for support. After the service, Frank took her other arm and we helped her walk to the diner where she had arranged a reception for everyone.

We didn't stay long. Doris was fading fast. I saw her talking to the two officers who'd questioned us the day we found out about the murders. As we helped her to the car, I asked if they had any new information. She shook her head and I didn't press her.

I was thankful Frank had driven. Doris sat in the back seat huddled under a blanket he'd put around her shoulders.

We stopped for gas just south of Fort Wayne. As we pulled into the station, a white compact car went past. I'd first noticed it when we'd left Wadesboro. It had been behind us as we took the ramp onto the highway. I saw brake lights come on as it pulled over onto the shoulder. It was too far away for me to see who was driving, but the kidnapper from the airport had driven a white compact. Maybe I was over-reacting, but what if I weren't and it was him?

I quickly got out of the car. Frank had finished pumping gas and was coming out of the station with three cups of coffee. I spoke softly so Doris wouldn't hear, "I think we're being followed. It's that white compact that just drove by. He's waiting for us about a half mile further on."

Frank was a rock. He didn't waste time asking questions, just nodded. We pulled around the back of the station and turned left onto a side road. After travelling west for a few miles, he turned left again and cut across a county road, until he came to a main road that went south in roughly the same direction as the highway.

Doris came to enough to ask, "Why are we going back a different way?"

"I'm taking a short cut, Doris. Trying to beat the traffic is all."

Satisfied, she leaned back in her seat and sipped her coffee.

We drove for a few more miles until we saw the signs for I-65. Frank followed that south until we neared Indianapolis and hit 465 over to I-74 and home. I watched the side and rear view mirrors, checked every road we passed, but saw no sign of the white car. We seemed to have lost him.

Or maybe I was becoming paranoid and I'd imagined the whole thing. Frank looked at me and raised an eyebrow. I shook my head and mouthed, "Later."

Doris was quiet for the next couple of weeks, but being Doris, she worked out her feelings by going through the apartment like a tornado, sorting and cleaning with a vengeance. I had promised her I would go through my wardrobe for any unwanted clothes she and Margaret could turn into costumes for the play. I'd found a few evening dresses I'd never wear again and was now going through my jewelry box. There were some outdated necklaces, a string of crystal beads, and at the back of the box, my wedding ring.

Originally, I had tossed it in the trash then retrieved it when I'd decided I couldn't let it go. I looked at it—a perfect circle—symbol of everlasting love. I tossed it on the discard pile. I didn't need it any more.

"You're throwing that away?"

"I don't want it, Doris."

"Then you mind if I take it? I save things for Enid. She makes those college things out of bits and bobs and she could use it."

"College things? Oh, you mean collages?"

"Yes, those collages. She takes all kinds of junk and makes things you wouldn't believe. You should see what she puts together."

As far as I was concerned, Enid was welcome to it.

I had talked to Ellie after she'd been told I was no longer a suspect. She'd apologized, but added, "Mom, you were going to be charged with attempted murder. What were we to think?"

Think? Maybe, that although her mother may have lost it when she'd found her husband having sex with his secretary—sorry, personal assistant—she wasn't capable of plotting to lure him to her apartment to try to kill him. That just maybe, Ellie could have asked me what happened that night instead of assuming the worst..

I was angry with Ellie. I was angry with Jack. But most of all I was angry with myself. Nobody decreed I had to be Caesar's wife. I could have gone back to school and worked on my degree. I could have done one of any number of things. Instead, I chose to become the perfect wife and mother, something I now bitterly regretted. Thirty wasted years I told myself—wasted on a useless, faithless man.

I accepted Ellie's apology but the rift was not bridged for either of us. I asked her why her father had been in my apartment. She professed not to know and trotted out the amnesia story.

"Right, he ends up in my apartment, gets his head bashed in, and has no idea of how or why he got there? Do his doctors have any idea when he's going to regain his memory?"

"Mom, I don't know, okay? I haven't talked to them."

She refused to discuss the subject again, which told me that Ellie didn't buy the amnesia story either but wouldn't admit it.

Chapter 13

Doris called me half-way through my shift at the library to tell me she was out of yeast and could I stop at the bakery on my way home to pick up a couple of loaves of bread. I didn't mind, though I usually tried to avoid our local bakery—the pastries were way too tempting.

I was outside the shop admiring a particularly fetching display of chocolate cream puffs, when I saw someone across the street staring at my reflection in the window. I felt rather than saw our eyes meet. His were hidden behind dark wrap-around sunglasses.

How could the kidnapper be in Shelbyville? I know we had eluded him on the way back from Charlie's funeral. On the drive home I'd barely taken my eyes off the rear and side view mirrors. Anyway, however he had found us, I had to somehow shake him off.

I saw him check traffic, then start across the street towards me. A car passed him honking loudly. He momentarily stopped and while his view of me was blocked, I ducked into the hair salon next to the bakery.

"Can you let me out your back door?"

The girl behind the reception desk stopped filing her nails and stared at me, open-mouthed. All six of the occupied chairs swiveled my way.

The closest of the beauticians started to shake her head. "Sorry, honey. That's only for employees."

I thought fast. "My ex-boyfriend is outside. We just broke up. He gets kind of violent sometimes. I don't want him to see me."

.The kidnapper from the airport had crossed the street and was outside the window looking around. He started to turn and I hastily ducked down behind the desk.

After a minute or two, the young receptionist whispered in my ear, "It's all right now. He went into the bakery. You want me to call the police?"

I shook my head. "I just need to get out of here before he sees me"

Maybe it was a woman thing—female solidarity—but suddenly everyone wanted to help.

The older, blonde beautician grabbed a ring of keys from under the counter. "Quick, this way—I'll unlock the door for you."

"Thank you so much."

She hugged me. "We've all been there, honey. Men can be real bastards sometimes. If he asks, we never saw you."

I slipped out the back door, and keeping a close watch behind me, turned left. I kept to the alleys and paralleled Main Street until I was north of our house, just where the road curved around. I quickly crossed the street, ran down the side of the building and climbed up the back stairs into the kitchen.

Doris was taking a pan out of the oven. She saw my face and almost dropped it

"Doris, I saw him."

"Him? Who? Who did you see?"

"The man from the airport. He's in Shelbyville."

The color drained from her face. She grabbed the back of a chair for support.

"Doris, we have to call the police."

"No. I'll take care of it." And she refused to say another word.

I should have gone with my first instinct. The next morning when I got up, Doris was gone.

Chapter 14

The sofa bed in the den was folded up. The cushions were plumped and neatly placed along the back. Her battered suitcase and old cream purse were gone. There was a note on the desk written in her spidery handwriting, *I'm going away for a while. Don't worry about me. There's lasagna in the fridge for your dinner; heat it up at 350, and we're almost out of coffee.*

I called everyone I could think of. Rose and Enid had not seen her leave. None of our library friends knew where she had gone. Our local cab company did not pick her up. I even ran across the alley to Mrs. Turner's cottage, but no cars or strangers lurking around the house had been logged into her notebook. There was nothing for it—I had to call the police.

No joy there—whack your cheating husband a couple of times with a golf club and half the Shelbyville Police Department show up with flashing lights and handcuffs—but ask them to find an eighty-year-old woman whom you knew was being stalked by a violent kidnapper—and they act as if it were an everyday occurrence.

The police officer taking the report had that 'I'm listening but don't give a crap' tone of voice. "Ma'am, you say Mrs. Weppler took all her belongings with her? That tells me she left voluntarily."

"No, there was this man at the airport who tried to pull her into his car, and he followed us back after her cousin's funeral. He was murdered—the cousin—not the man. Then I saw him outside the bakery near the square—the man, that is—and he tried to follow me."

I was trying to frame my narrative in a way the officer could understand, but failing miserably. "When I told Doris—Mrs. Weppler—I could tell she was upset, but she said she'd take care of it. What if he came back and kidnapped her again?"

I may not have been totally coherent, maybe even babbling a little, but he didn't even pretend to listen. He interrupted me with a curt, "I'll file the report and we'll let you know when we hear something. Ma'am, let's face it, she's not a relative of yours."

But she was. She wasn't exactly my mother or grandmother, but family isn't always the people who are related to you by birth. And even though she was as tough as an old boot, I knew she was terrified of the strange man at the airport. I couldn't leave her out there scared and alone. I had to do something. I took a deep breath and reluctantly called Sam.

He answered with a terse, "Detective Williamson."

"It's Kate, Kate Conley."

There was complete silence then, "What can I do for you?"

"It's Doris, Mrs. Weppler, the woman who lives with me. She's missing. I wouldn't bother you with this, but nobody in your department seems in the slightest bit concerned and I think she might be in danger."

"Why? What makes you think that?"

I told him about seeing the kidnapper outside the bakery and how he had come after me.

"Are you at home right now?"

"Yes."

"I'll be over in thirty minutes."

Sure enough, exactly thirty minutes later there was a polite rap at my door.

"Detective Williamson, Mrs. Conley." Which was, I thought, pretty formal for a man who'd seen me naked. I took a deep breath and opened my door to the one man I had planned to never see again.

Sam wasn't alone. The female officer, who had brought me tea the night I'd found Jack, was with him. We stood there for a moment, Sam looking anywhere but at my face. There was an awkward silence until I remembered my manners and invited them to sit.

There was another silence. The policewoman cleared her throat and looked at Sam.

He gave a start, almost stammered and said, "You have some concerns regarding Mrs. Weppler?"

This was excruciatingly embarrassing. I figured it was for Sam, too. The tips of his ears were red and he didn't seem to know what to do with his hands.

I took a deep breath, "As I told you on the phone, she's missing. She left without telling me, either late last night or early this morning, and nobody seems to know where she is."

I showed him Doris' note and added that she had taken all her belongings with her.

"Why do you think she's in danger?"

"After her cousin's funeral..." I broke off. "He was murdered..."

Sam stopped me. "I know about the murders in Wadesboro. Go on..."

"There was a car following us when we left after the funeral. It looked like the same one from the airport..."

"Tell me about the car at the airport."

"I told you, Sam. That night at Luigi's..." The color rushed into my face. "I meant, I told you how I met Doris on the plane. Then at the airport some man tried to force her into his car. She said he mistook her for someone else."

"And the car that followed you was the same car?"

"I'm not certain but it looked like it."

"When you called to report Mrs. Weppler missing, you said the kidnapper from the airport was in Shelbyville."

"Yes."

"Have you seen him anywhere near your house?"

"No." I explained about slipping out the back door of the beauty salon. "I kept to the alleys. I'm certain he didn't see where I went. When I got home, I told Doris he was in Shelbyville. I could tell she was upset but she wouldn't talk about it. I never thought she would just leave. I should have called the police right away."

My voice started to shake. Sam looked at the policewoman.

She handed me a bunch of tissues that she took from her purse. "How about a cup of tea, ma'am?" She went into the kitchen, and I heard water running and the rattle of cups.

Sam and I sat in silence. Finally, I plucked up enough courage to speak. "Look, I know we both would prefer that night never had happened so can we please agree, we were drunk, it was a big mistake, and never mention it again?"

The color spread all the way down Sam's ears. "I felt terrible about what happened. I never should have let it get that far. I did call to apologize, but you wouldn't answer the phone."

"I know. It was too embarrassing. I don't usually get drunk and bed the first man I see. It was easier to pretend it never happened. Please, can we just forget it?"

The policewoman came back with my tea. She looked from Sam to me, and wisely put the cup on the coffee table and took up her seat again.

Sam had a few more questions before he left. He promised to contact me as soon as he learned anything new.

He stopped by the apartment a couple of days later to tell me a woman answering Doris' description had bought a ticket to Miami Beach at the Indianapolis Greyhound Bus station.

"However, when we looked at the security cameras we didn't see her get on the bus. There was no trace of her at Union Station, and she hadn't checked into any of the local hotels. Mrs. Weppler seems to have done a pretty good job of disappearing."

"But that man...."

"Don't worry; if he's in Shelbyville, we'll find him."

He paused in the doorway. I waited for him to leave. Finally, he said quietly, "Kate, I want you to know I don't usually get drunk and bed the first woman I see, either."

And he quickly left before I could answer.

Chapter 15

I heard nothing from Doris. I also heard nothing from Sam who sent any updates through his police officer partner, whose name I learned was Martha. She checked in with me every few days to let me know they had nothing new on Doris' disappearance, but were still investigating.

By now, our whole group knew that Doris was missing. Stephen was surprisingly supportive. Though he'd been doing my hair for years, I can't say I really knew him. He was a brittle-edged person with a biting tongue, and I was always wary of him. I could never understand how he and warm, cuddly Sebastian could be partners. Doris seemed to love him, and for his part, he seemed as fond of her.

"Kate, don't worry about Doris. She's smart enough to take care of herself. She'll turn up one of these days. Wait and see."

I hoped he was right. Martha told me the kidnapper had left Shelbyville, but they knew where he was and were watching him.

I'd just got home after an exhausting rehearsal one night when the phone rang. I didn't recognize the caller ID, but picked up anyway.

A tentative voice said, "Is this Kate Conley?"

"Yes. Who is this?"

"Walter, Walter Moore. I'm your husband's dentist. Sorry, I mean your former husband."

I vaguely remembered Walter. He wasn't a friend but we had moved in the same circles, and his wife had been on the museum board with me.

"I'm calling to see if you and I could have dinner sometime."

"Dinner? But you're..?"

"Divorced. I mean, I'm divorced—my wife and I. And you and your husband. We're all divorced."

I was speechless. Taking my silence for consent, he blurted out, "How about tomorrow night?"

My brain and tongue froze. "Well..."

"Great. I'll pick you up around seven." And he hung up.

My first date in thirty years! There was only one person to call.

According to Sylvia, I had done everything wrong.

"Kate, never let a man pick you up at your house. You always drive yourself and meet him at the restaurant. That way if he's boring or a bit creepy, you can make some excuse and leave."

Also, accepting a last minute dinner date for a Friday night made me look desperate.

"What should I have done?"

"You should have told him you weren't free and suggested a Monday or Tuesday evening instead. Better still, you should have made it lunch—less pressure that way."

"But I hardly remember him. I was surprised to get his call. I didn't know what to say. I'm not sure I want to go."

"No, go! But you can always call me. If it doesn't turn out well, you can ditch him and I'll take you home."

I wasn't certain if that was reassuring or not.

Walter turned up on time. I watched for the car and ran down to meet him because Sylvia said not to let him into the apartment. She also said don't dress up as if it's something special—so I wore slacks and a casual jacket.

Before she hung up she said, "Be sure you don't let him pay for your meal."

I hadn't even thought about who pays. "Because?"

"Because you don't want to be obligated in any way."

Obligated? Had Sam felt I was obligated because he'd bought the wine on that disastrous evening? Something else to worry about! Dating seemed to be a minefield. When had the rules become so complicated?

There aren't that many decent restaurants in Shelbyville, and Luigi's was a favorite of half the population of the county. So it was inevitable, the way my luck was going, that it would be Walter's choice.

Unfortunately, that evening, it was also the choice of Detective Sam Williamson. Luigi seated us two tables in front of him and he stared directly at me. He did not look happy. Well, too bad, I didn't choose the restaurant. And I wasn't happy to see him either.

Walter was holding my chair for me. He was the kind of man who liked to hold things—chairs, the car door—even my jacket. It was irritating. I wanted to tell him I wasn't exactly helpless. Luigi picked up on the awkward situation. After all, the last time I was there I was with Sam and we both had had way too much to drink.

"Is this table all right? You could sit in the other dining room if you prefer."

But, of course, Walter was oblivious. "No, this is fine."

With a worried glance at me, Luigi placed the menus in front of us with his usual elaborate flourish and departed.

So here I was in hell again, and the evening had just begun. Every time I looked up, Sam was glaring at me. Even when I made a conscious effort to avoid looking at him, I could feel his eyes on me.

And Walter was just plain irritating. First he made a big production out of choosing the wine, taking far too long to do the sniffing, tasting thing. Next, even though I told him I wanted only sparkling water, he insisted on pouring a glass of wine for me, which I left untouched and which he kept offering. Then he tried to order for both of us and was visibly irritated when I ordered for myself. The evening almost ended when I told the waiter it would be separate checks.

"When I invite a woman to dinner I expect to pay the bill."

"And when I go to dinner with someone I hardly know, I expect to pay for myself."

It escalated from there and I started to gather up my purse and jacket. "Perhaps you'd prefer to eat alone?"

"No Kate, please don't go. I'm sorry. This is my first date since the divorce and I'm not sure of the protocol."

I could relate. Dating was nerve wracking.

"Can we start over? I think maybe I'm trying too hard."

So we did, and I totally got what Sylvia meant when she said—recently divorced—too needy.

This wasn't a date—it was a therapy session and I was the therapist—and it went on for hours—boring, interminable, never ending hours! Walter poured out his heart to me in one long monologue which took up the whole meal. I had his first meeting with his wife, through courtship and wedding, with my antipasto. The marriage and its breakdown took up most of the chicken piccata. Even though I love Luigi's tiramisu, I skipped dessert, thinking it would shorten the narrative. It didn't. The agonizing heartbreak, excruciatingly painful divorce was accompanied by our after dinner coffee—and my role, I realized, was to sit there, listen, and make the occasional sympathetic comment. I was bitterly regretting my decision to not drink wine.

I briefly escaped to the bathroom where I considered banging my head against the wall. But there were other people there so I couldn't. I almost called Sylvia but decided Walter was so pathetic I couldn't abandon him.

The waiter was refilling my coffee when I returned to the table. I was hoping this hellish meal was almost over and I could make my escape, when I saw Sam check his phone. He looked directly at me, then dropped his eyes and called the waiter over. The next time I looked up he was heading for the exit.

It took another thirty minutes and an argument over the bill, before we finally got out of the restaurant. During that time, I had committed to another date with Walter. I was able to beg off dinner, citing a heavy rehearsal schedule, but he grabbed my hand saying, "Kate, you don't know what a relief it is for me to be able to confide in someone as understanding as you. I know you're busy, but surely you can spare an hour to have lunch with me?"

And dumb old me, I couldn't come up with a single excuse. So I was stuck with therapy session number two.

We drove in silence to my place. Walter was happy to have another date lined up, and I was silently pondering how to get out of it.

We turned the corner onto my street. Three police cars, complete with flashing lights, were parked outside the house. I saw Rose and Enid on the front porch, talking to Martha. Sam was there too questioning some of the neighbors.

I was out of the car almost before it stopped. "I'd better see what's wrong."

"Let me come with you."

"No, my neighbors are right there, and the police. I'll be fine."

But, of course, he was already around the front of the car. "Goodnight Kate, I had a wonderful evening."

There was an awkward pause. He leaned towards me and I started backing up, which is why his wet kiss landed in the region of my left ear. With a hurried goodnight, I almost ran towards the house.

Chapter 16

"You've been broken into, but it's all right; he didn't get anything."

That was my greeting from Enid and Rose, as I hurried up the front walk. I looked around. Sam caught my eye and walked over. "Can we go inside?"

"What happened?"

"Evidently someone broke into your apartment through your front door. Your neighbor saw it as she was retrieving her cat from the hallway."

Rose's words tripped over themselves, "I went up the front stairs to get Petey, and I saw a guy in a dark hoodie, bending down doing something to your lock. I yelled for Enid to call the police. He kicked your door open, ran into the apartment and got out through the back. Mrs. Turner saw him run down the alley."

She paused to take a breath, "Come on up. We'll show you what he did."

I followed Enid and Rose up the front staircase, with Sam trailing behind. The jamb of my beautiful old door was splintered and there was a long gash in its gleaming, mahogany finish. Two officers were coming down from the sullen tenant's apartment above me.

"Nobody home up there, sir."

We went inside. Apart from the front door being kicked in, nothing seemed to be disturbed.

"We've contacted our landlord and he's trying to get someone to fix your door." Enid shook her head ruefully, "It's hard to find a locksmith at this time of night."

Martha came in. "I've been trying too, but no luck anywhere. Your landlord says he's got someone who'll be here first thing in the morning. Now he's looking for a carpenter who can repair your front door."

It took another hour before the police were totally done. Enid offered me their spare room until the door was fixed but it was past midnight and the locksmith wouldn't arrive until eight in the morning.

"Thanks, I'll just nap on the couch for now. The door will be fixed in a few hours."

Actually, I planned to sit up for the rest of the night keeping watch.

"All right, but we'll be downstairs if you need us."

Finally, everyone was gone except Sam. I waited for him to leave. He cleared his throat nervously. "If you don't mind, I think I should stay until the locksmith gets here. Your place isn't exactly secure, and if that guy comes back—you know—the police will be on the premises."

I didn't want to spend the next few hours on my couch nervously listening for an intruder. Neither did I want Sam in my apartment overnight. I started to object but Sam decided for me. He took a chair and jammed it under the door knob. "That will have to do for now."

There was an awkward silence. He went into the kitchen to check that everything was secure. I trailed after him. He examined the lock on the back door then stood there as if he had something else to say. Finally he asked, "Have you heard anything from Mrs. Weppler?"

"No, nothing. I would like to know she's safe."

"There have been no reports of," he broke off, "sorry, that was insensitive, I mean…."

"You mean no bodies of eighty-year-old women have turned up."

He sat down at the table with me. "Look, Kate, Mrs. Weppler seems to be very resourceful. I'm sure when it's safe she'll be back." He added, "Can I ask you a question? How long have you been dating Walter Moore?"

I would have told him it was just one date, the date from hell never to be repeated, except of course it would be, but I didn't get the chance. My phone rang. It was Walter.

"I just heard it was a break-in. Don't worry about anything. I'll be right over."

By the time I'd convinced him I already had police protection and he wasn't needed, Sam was bedded down on my couch. He didn't reply to my whispered goodnight.

Chapter 17

It took me a long time to go to sleep that night. Consequently, I slept late and it was past eight when I finally woke. I dressed hurriedly, hoping to be up before the locksmith arrived, but when I entered the kitchen, he was hard at work. Sam was sitting at the table drinking coffee.

"Morning, ma'am, your..." he looked at Sam, not sure how to refer to him, then decided to leave it alone. "I'm almost finished with this, but you'll have to get someone to repair your front door to make it totally secure. The owner wants me to replace the locks on all the apartments and the entry door downstairs. It should have been done before this. These locks are original to the house, and with a little jiggling, the same key opens all three doors. I'll be back with your new keys when I'm done."

Sam looked as if he'd been up all night. I offered him more coffee. He shook his head. "There'll be someone by in the next hour to fix the jamb on your front door. I asked your landlord about installing a security system. He said no. I need to talk to you about something but I have to get into the precinct. I'll stop by later."

"Wait. Did you hear what the locksmith said about how the same key could fit all three apartment doors?"

That seemed to get his attention.

"Doesn't that mean anyone in the house could have opened my door and let Jack in the night he was attacked?"

Sam paused. "That's something we'll discuss later. I have to go."

I thought of the almost two weeks of daily interrogations after Jack had been found lying on my kitchen floor, and how Sam and the younger detective kept insisting I must have given Jack a key to my apartment. Yes, we would discuss it later.

The carpenter came and fixed the door jamb. He also refinished the wood so the ugly gash disappeared. "Ma'am, if you could leave the door open until this evening that will give the varnish time to dry completely."

My phone rang. It was Walter. "Walter, I'm in the middle of something here. I'll talk to you later." And I hung up.

It immediately rang again. This time I told him I was too busy to talk to him and hung up again. After that, I checked caller ID, and let it go to voice-mail.

Frank and Sebastian stopped in on the way to rehearsal. Stephen called wanting details of the break-in. Enid and Rose came up from downstairs with a bottle of wine. Sylvia brought some chocolate cream puffs from the bakery. I checked the freezer and found a chicken casserole that Doris had left. It was a regular open house—quite literally, since I couldn't close my apartment door until the paint was dry.

Sebastian put his arm around my shoulder. "Kate, you've been through enough today. You can skip rehearsal tonight, but Hell Week starts tomorrow."

"What is Hell Week?" I'd heard everyone talking about it, but no one had told me what it was.

He laughed. "Just what it sounds like. From now on we rehearse every night until we open. I'm giving you a break tonight, but after this, I expect you at the theater with the rest of the cast. Get plenty of sleep; you'll need it."

The play was scheduled to run for three weekends with matinees on the first two Sunday afternoons. I was excited and nervous at the same time. I wondered if Doris was thinking about the play. She had loved working on the costumes.

After everyone left, I loaded the dishwasher and went into the living room to check for stray plates. As I turned the corner, I ran into someone standing quietly by the door watching me. For one panic-stricken moment, I thought the burglar had returned. I almost screamed before I realized it was Walter.

"What are you doing here? You almost gave me a heart attack."

"You didn't answer my phone calls. I thought I'd better come over to see if you're all right"

"How did you get in?"

"Your friends were leaving, and they held the downstairs door for me when I told them I was coming to check on you."

"Walter, I'm tired. I don't feel like having more company. Please leave and don't stop in again unless you call first."

He said stiffly, "I'm sorry. I was concerned when you didn't answer my calls."

"If I didn't answer it's because you called too many times so I let them go to voice mail."

I saw something flare in his eyes. He reached out and grabbed my arm. I was trying to pull away when a voice said, "Is everything all right here?" Sam was standing in the doorway with Martha behind him.

My heart was pounding. "Yes. Walter was just leaving."

He dropped his hand from my arm. "I'll call you tomorrow."

Martha said smoothly, "I'll walk down with you, sir, and make sure the outside door is locked behind you. It was standing open when we came in." I watched her follow Walter out the door.

"Kate, what just happened?"

"I'm not sure." I was shaken. For a brief moment, I felt Walter had almost threatened me. "I guess when I didn't return Walter's phone calls, he became worried and stopped by. My neighbors let him in downstairs and my door was open because of the wet paint. He startled me and I wasn't very polite."

"You need to be more careful about who you date."

I couldn't believe what I heard. "Did you just tell me who I should date?"

Sam's ears were red again. "No, I was just saying maybe you shouldn't go out with the first man who asks you. Not everyone is as they seem."

The first man who asks me? What made Sam think Walter was the first man who asked me? He was, if you didn't count a drunken Sam, but how dare he assume that?

I tried a little deep breathing and calmly said, "I think that's my affair not yours." Then I wondered if "affair" was the wisest word choice.

Martha came back at that moment and averted what was shaping up to be a major argument. She was trying to coax the most pathetic dog I'd ever seen, into the living room. The dog sat down on his haunches inside the doorway and refused to move. She looked to Sam for help, but he'd turned away and was staring, stony faced, at the far wall.

She gave an exasperated shake of her head. "Kate, this is Digger. He's a stray who's been hanging around the station for the last few days. He doesn't seem to belong to anyone so we've been feeding him." She looked at Sam again, picked up on the tension in the room, and went on, "We…I thought that since you don't have an alarm system, he might be protection for you. A barking dog can scare off intruders."

Digger was the most nondescript dog I'd ever seen. He had droopy ears like a basset, a rough brownish grayish coat like a terrier and a head too small for his body. His one asset was his big sad eyes. They were irresistible.

"We've been told to get rid of him. I can't have him in my apartment, so we thought you might want to take him until we can find a permanent home for him." She waited hopefully then hurried on, "He's a really nice guy. He's been fixed, has all his shots and we took him to the groomer today, so he's clean."

I looked down at Digger. He shook all over and his skinny tail was firmly tucked between his back legs. They had to be kidding about the protection part!

He looked up at me with his mournful eyes. Did I say they were irresistible?

"Okay. He can stay—for now."

Chapter 18

It took a few days before Digger's tail came out from between his legs, and a few more before it started wagging. But once he felt at home in my apartment, he stayed glued to my side. When I left for rehearsal or the library, he followed me to the door and watched me go, his sad eyes pleading with me to stay.

When I came home, he was there behind the door, waiting for it to open so he could greet me with sloppy dog kisses and a tail thumping so hard I had to move everything off the end tables. He slept next to me on my bed with his head on the pillow, but stayed off the rest of the furniture. The only vice he had was digging up the back yard. As fast as he dug a hole, I refilled it. But I was always one hole behind and the yard was beginning to look pretty chewed up. Digger was well named.

The one thing he wasn't was protection. He was terrified of Petey—Rose and Enid's cat. If Petey was on the back stairs, Digger refused to pass him and we had to take the front stairs to go outside. He liked me, Sam, and Martha. Anyone else sent him slinking off to another room, where he crawled under any piece of furniture he could find with just his tail sticking out. He stayed there until everyone left.

Hell Week wasn't hell; it was sheer, unadulterated fun. I loved my slutty maid's costume. Stephen had pinned a blond fall into my hair and teased it up high.

By the time Thursday came around, I wasn't tired but exhilarated.

Dress rehearsal was long and complicated. Light cues were missed, sound cues were late, actors muffed their lines and missed entrances. Even sweet-tempered Sebastian was getting a little cranky. Our perennial whiner, Mark, was trying to tell him it would be much funnier if I banged the plate down in front of him, instead of Sylvia.

"That way, Sebastian, the laughs would start earlier, and you know I can do a great double-take…"

"We're not changing it at dress rehearsal. It stays the way I blocked it."

Mark stomped off. Sebastian rolled his eyes at me. "He's going to suggest it to you next. Just ignore him and do it the way we rehearsed."

Poor Mark, he was one of the weaker members of the cast, but it didn't stop him from trying to pad his part as much as possible. Usually, we would have met up at the Pancake House after rehearsal, but it was past midnight and we were all too tired.

"Goodnight. See you tomorrow."

Everyone piled into their cars anxious to get home. Mine was parked under a tree at the far corner of the rutted lot. I'd just opened the door when I felt a hand on my arm. I gave a startled squeak and turned, heart racing. It was Walter.

"I know you've been busy with the play so I haven't called you. But I want you to know I'll be there for opening night. As soon as the play is over, we'll go out to dinner again, but in the meantime let's fix a day to meet for lunch."

His hand was still on my arm. I shook it off. He grabbed me by the shoulders and turned me around so I faced him.

"Let go." I tried to pull away, but Walter held on tighter.

Then I heard Mark's plaintive voice, "Kate, do you have a few minutes? I have a great idea for the dining room scene."

Walter dropped his arms. Mark was hot-footing it across the parking lot toward me. Normally, I would have jumped in the car and made some excuse to avoid him. Instead, I moved to him and took hold of his sleeve. "Let me give you a ride home. We can talk on the way."

And I hustled a bewildered Mark into the car, clicked the doors locked, and backed out of the space. Walter was standing in front of the car as I started to move forward. I almost ran over him, but he moved just in time. When I looked in the rear-view mirror, he was still standing there, staring.

Mark babbled away, "We'd get a lot more laughs out of that scene if we did it my way...."

I let his voice wash over me. This was definitely getting out of hand. I needed another talk with Sylvia.

Chapter 19

It was the opening night of the play. I was terrified. I wasn't an actor—I'd never appeared onstage in my entire life. What made me think I could carry off the slutty maid role with a skirt practically up to my thigh, push-up bra, big hair and gaudy make-up? What if there were people from the museum board or country club in the audience?

I hadn't told Ellie about the show, but she called anyway. "You never told me you were in a play. I had to find out from the newspaper."

"It's just a small part—a maid—I don't even have any lines. That's why I didn't mention it."

That, plus Ellie would be less than thrilled to see her mother onstage in the outrageous costume Margaret and Stephen had created for me.

"This weekend is sold out. Andrew and I had to make reservations for next Saturday."

A reprieve! I couldn't deal with stage fright and a disapproving daughter. And I could only imagine what my straight-laced son-in-law would make of my performance.

I wasn't the only one suffering from first night nerves. Mark wasn't speaking to me since I'd squelched his ideas from the night before, but he couldn't hide his strained face and trembling lips. Sebastian paced like an expectant father and Sylvia positively shook.

"Kate, you have flowers. Are you all decent?" We yelled *yes*, and Frank came into the women's dressing room, carrying a bouquet of red roses.

"Who are they from?" Everybody crowded around. I looked at the card. There was no name. They were sent from the florist across from the theater, and the message simply said, "Break a leg." The note was signed, "From your secret admirer." The only admirer I had was Walter, and he was hardly a secret. Still they were lovely and took my mind off the cold knot forming in my stomach.

Our little assistant stage manager rapped on the door, "Places everyone." It was too late for escape. The house lights went down. There was an expectant hush. The stage lights came on, and the curtain went up

I stood in the wings waiting for my entrance. I heard my cue, froze, and somehow propelled myself onstage. The lights almost blinded me, but I could feel a wave of interest coming from the audience as I made my entrance. I dropped the plate in front of Mark and worked my way down the table. Thank god I had no lines. I wouldn't have remembered one of them. I slammed the plate down in front of Sylvia. She screamed, and I got my first big laugh. I looked at the audience, rolled my eyes, mouthed, *silly cow*, and got an even bigger one. From then on it was pure euphoria. I came offstage to a round of applause and couldn't wait for my next entrance.

Sebastian gave me a big hug. "You got an exit round—they're loving it. Keep it going."

And I did. The rest of the evening was magic. I know this wasn't Broadway. And most of the audience was made up of friends and family who were going to laugh and applaud anyway. It was a strictly amateur production of a not very good play, and it was far from perfect. Mark got his zipper stuck and had to make his next entrance with his shirt pulled out to cover his open fly. Judging by the muffled giggles coming from the front row, he was unsuccessful. In the excitement, our little ASM forgot to make the tea for the poisoning scene and Sylvia had to pretend to pour the tea which the actors had to pretend to drink. But the audience didn't seem to care. We were getting great laughs in all the right places, plus some where we hadn't expected any.

It was so much more fun than I'd ever imagined. I finally understood why actors went through the agony of endless rehearsals, the drudgery of learning lines, and the terror of stage fright. It was for this feeling of love and approval from the audience. I felt powerful up there on stage. The audience laughed if I so much as raised an eyebrow or twitched a hip. It was heady stuff.

We had rehearsed our curtain call the night before. Mark wasn't happy that I was placed after the minor characters and before the leads.

"She doesn't even have any lines," he was heard to say. But again, Sebastian prevailed.

The audience was enthusiastic, clapping loudly for everyone. I ran out on stage to take my bow and the applause swelled. A few people stood up. Then the leads came out one by one, with Sylvia last and the whole audience was on their feet. We took eight standing ovations before Sebastian rang down the curtain for the last time.

The opening night party was in the lobby. It was packed. I threaded my way through the crowd toward the table holding the champagne and hors d'oeuvres. Complete strangers were stopping me to tell me how good I had been and how much they enjoyed the play. I was practically floating until I turned, champagne in hand, to find Walter at my side.

He put a possessive arm around my shoulder. "When you're through here, I have a late dinner reservation for us."

I shook him off. "I never said I was going to dinner with you. I have other plans."

My phone rang. I pulled away from him, turned and to my surprise, bumped into a grim-looking Detective Sam Williamson. He steadied me before I tripped.

I turned back to my phone. "Hello?" I had to repeat myself. I couldn't hear over the noisy, opening night crowd.

A quavering little voice said, "Can you come get me?"

It was Doris.

Chapter 20

"Are you all right? Hold on a minute." Walter was at my side again so I escaped to the one place he couldn't follow—the ladies bathroom. It was empty.

"Where are you?"

"I'm in Danville. Only I need you to come get me." Doris sounded panicked.

"Doris, tell me exactly where you are."

She gave me directions to a diner on Main Street. Danville was about an hour away. I told her I'd get there as fast as I could and she was to wait for me.

"Okay, but I don't know when they close."

"Just wait, I'll be as quick as I can."

I came out of the restroom to find Sam standing to one side, waiting for me. Walter was lurking in the background. I grabbed Sam and dragged him to a quiet corner of the room away from everyone.

"It's Doris. She's in Danville and she wants me to come get her."

Sam wasted no time. "All right; let's go."

He took my arm and led me out to the parking lot. Sylvia gave me a thumbs-up as I passed. Walter trailed us to the door. Sam turned and looked at him. He dropped his eyes and almost slunk back into the theater.

Sam drove, for which I was thankful. "Did Mrs. Weppler give you any indication of how or why she was there?"

"No, but she definitely sounded scared."

He must have taken a shortcut because we pulled up outside the diner in a little over thirty minutes. Doris was sitting in a corner booth by herself. She paled when she saw Sam.

"You shouldn't have brought him."

"Doris, it's all right. We've come to take you home."

"No, I can't come back yet. Not until it's safe. You'll have to take me somewhere else."

I sat next to her and put my arms around her. "Doris, you have to tell me. Why is that man following you?"

Tears welled up in her eyes and spilled down her wrinkled cheeks. Finally, she choked out the words, "I think he was sent to kill me."

I held her as she wept silently into a paper napkin.

The waitress came over. "Is everything all right?"

"Yes, she's had some bad news."

"Oh, honey, let me get you some more coffee and a piece of pie." The waitress hurried away and came back with a piece of pie for Doris, and coffee all round. "Call me if you need anything else."

The pie helped. Doris pulled herself together. "I don't know where to start."

"Start at the beginning and take your time," Sam said gently.

She took a deep breath, "It's about my son. Me and Otis never had but the one child. Tommy wasn't interested in farming, didn't have the knack for it, but we didn't care about that. Farming's not for everyone. He wanted to go to college, so we sent him to Indiana University, where Charlie went to school."

Her mouth tightened when she said her cousin's name. "Then he wanted to go to Honolulu for his graduate work, so we paid for him to go there too. But nothing was ever enough—he wanted a new car, a bigger allowance—by the time he was done with school, we was tired of supporting him. So we told him he'd have to get a job like everyone else"

Her voice trembled, but she pulled herself together and went on, "He was angry. He called Otis a stupid, hick farmer, and Otis said a hick farmer who's smart enough not to give any more money to a lazy son like you. Anyway, when he realized we meant it and he wasn't getting anything more, he broke off all contact with us."

She stopped to drain her coffee and Sam signaled a refill for her. The motherly waitress bustled over with the coffee pot, anxious to help. Sam was patient. He let Doris tell the story in her own way, with no pressure from him.

"When Otis passed, I sold the farm and all the land. I was going to move back to Wadesboro to be near Charlie. Then out of the blue, Tommy called. He said he was sorry we had become estranged and life was too short to bear grudges. Now I was alone why didn't I come to stay with him and meet his new wife?"

She gave a shuddering sigh. "I didn't even know he was married. I wanted to believe he meant it, that he'd changed, but it was only about the money; that's all he wanted from me. They was nice at first; then they started in on me. That woman said I should let Tommy take care of my business affairs. It was too much for an old woman like me."

She gave one of her sniffs. "As if he could handle money. When I said no, they started threatening me. Tommy said he would have me declared incompetent and have me committed in one of them asylums if I didn't sign the papers they had drawn up."

"When did you decide to leave?"

"As soon as I realized they was never going to stop until they got what they wanted. That's when I packed my suitcase and called a cab. I didn't think they were going to let me go. Tommy's wife pushed me down into a chair at the kitchen table and shoved a pen in my hand. She put the papers under my nose and told me to sign them. Instead, I ripped them up and threw them in her face. I told them I was going to leave everything to my cousin Charlie, and it would be a cold day in hell before they ever got one penny from me. She slapped me across the face."

She started shaking again. "If the cab driver hadn't come to the front door right then, I don't know what would have happened. Tommy got real ugly. He told me I'd regret not giving him the money. As I went out the door he screamed—you'll be sorry for this old woman. I spent the night in a hotel next to the airport and caught the first flight out in the morning."

Sam took her wrinkled hands in his. "You should have gone to the police. We could have helped you."

She said in a small voice, "I couldn't believe Tommy would...I needed to be sure. When that man tried to push me into his car at the airport, I told myself he had mistaken me for someone else. And then Kate and I went to Wadesboro, and I found out Charlie had been killed." She dropped her head and took a deep breath. "I tried to tell myself it was nothing to do with me, that it was just a chance robbery, but deep down I knew it had to be Tommy and that woman. When the man from the airport turned up in Shelbyville, I decided to leave so he'd go away and nobody else would be hurt."

I put my arm around her shoulder. "Doris, you should have told me this before."

"It was too hard. I still can't believe Tommy would have someone killed just for money. But nothing else makes sense does it?" The tears came thick and fast now. "He's my son—how could he want me dead?"

Sam cleared his throat. He waited until Doris recovered a little, then asked, "So where did you go? Where have you been all this time?"

"I've been staying in Lafayette."

Lafayette was a college town, about an hour and a half north of Indianapolis.

She gave a big sigh. "I don't want to get anyone in trouble...."

Sam assured her that he just needed to know where she had been and that no one was in trouble.

"Kate, when you told me that man was in Shelbyville, I called Stephen. He picked me up late that night and drove me up to Lafayette to stay with his friend, Phil. I've been in Phil's apartment all this time."

"So you never bought a ticket to Florida?" Sam asked.

Doris looked guilty. "No, that was Margaret. I knew Kate would call the police, so I had Margaret buy that ticket at the bus station to cover my tracks. We look alike so if the cameras caught her, you'd think it was me, and if that man came poking around, he'd think I went to Florida."

I saw Sam hide a smile. "Well, you had us all fooled. Now, why did you leave the apartment in Lafayette, and how did you get here?"

Doris had recovered her composure, but she didn't seem to want to answer Sam's question. "Could I have another piece of pie?"

Sam signaled the waitress by pointing to Doris' empty plate. "Tell me why you left and how you got to Danville."

The waitress hurried over with the pie. Doris made a pretense of eating, but after pushing it around her plate for a few minutes, she put down her fork and finally answered him.

"This morning, I was looking out the front window of Phil's apartment. That man, the one who tried to drag me into his car at the airport, came to the complex and I saw him go into the office...."

"Wait a minute, you're saying the man who tried to kidnap you at the airport, the same man who followed us back to Shelbyville after your cousin's funeral, was at the apartments in Lafayette?"

Doris looked at me. "He followed us back from Charlie's funeral, Kate?"

"I didn't tell you because we took a different way home and I thought we'd lost him."

She took a moment to digest this. Then she shook her head and said, "Anyway, I don't know how he found me, but he was there."

Sam interrupted, "Had you left the apartment at any time or contacted anyone?"

"There was only one time I went out, and I made sure it was after dark."

"Where did you go?"

"To the liquor store across the street. I asked the girl if I could use their phone if I paid for the call. I didn't want to use the one in the apartment in case they traced it."

"Who did you call?" Sam asked quietly.

"My son. I wanted to ask him whether he had hired someone to kill Charlie and me. I had to know for sure."

She looked at Sam. "He wasn't there so I didn't leave a message. But it couldn't have been the call. On the police shows you have to keep someone on the line for at least three minutes before they can trace it and I hung up right away."

"There's caller ID, Doris. He could have got the address through the phone number you called from."

She hung her head. "I didn't think of that."

"Okay, so we know that your son or his wife could have traced your call to the liquor store. And we know the man from the airport may have been checking the apartments because they were right across the street. Now tell me how you got to Danville?"

Doris was silent. Her eyes shifted frantically around the diner as if seeking help. Finding none, she finally blurted out, "I stole a car."

Sam and I stared at each other. He was as dumbfounded as I was.

Doris' hands started to shake. "The woman in the next apartment to Phil's always starts her car and lets it warm up for a few minutes before she leaves for work. When I saw that man go into the office, I knew I had to get out of there before he found me. The car was unlocked. I got in and drove away."

She looked at Sam. "I'm real sorry; I suppose you'll have to arrest me now."

"Doris, how could you get to Danville? You can't drive. You don't even have a driver's license."

"I never needed a license because Otis always drove the car, but it doesn't mean I can't drive, Kate. I've been driving tractors and trucks on the farm since I was old enough to see over the dash, just never on the road. It wasn't too hard on the freeway except everyone was going real fast, but the traffic got busy when I got close to Indianapolis and I must have taken a wrong turn. Then it started getting dark and I was driving for a long time and the car was getting low on gas. I don't know how I ended up in Danville."

"Where is the car now?"

"I thought I'd better get rid of it so no one could trace me. I turned off Main Street a couple of blocks back and parked behind a dentist's office. I wiped it down good to get rid of my fingerprints, and I tried to make sure I didn't leave any DNA behind. Are you going to take me in?"

Sam took her wrinkled hand in his. "I think you've been through enough for tonight. And since I haven't seen the car, we'll leave it to the dentist to report it to the local police. I'm sure they'll get it back to the rightful owner."

"What about not having a driver's license?"

"I didn't see you drive the car. So I can't arrest you for that."

Doris heaved a sigh of relief, then. "But won't they see me on the traffic cameras and put me on them machines for face recognition stuff?"

"Nobody is going to check traffic cams for a stolen car which has been recovered. Now we have to find a safe place for you to stay for the next few days."

I called Frank. I know I woke him but he told us to bring Doris over, and he would make sure she stayed out of sight until it was safe.

Chapter 21

I had barely dragged myself out of bed the next morning when the phone rang. It was Walter. "I just had to tell you how wonderful you were last night. I never go to the theater, but I'm definitely going to come to everything you're in. How about lunch today if you're not too tired after the play last night?"

Might as well get it over with. I'd talked to Sylvia and she told me the next time I met Walter I shouldn't give him a chance to talk, but drone on endlessly about my own divorce.

"Be sure and tell him how you attacked your ex-husband with a golf club and put him in the hospital. It might be a good idea to bring up your stay in the psych ward too. If that doesn't scare him off, just tell him it isn't working for you."

When I said I felt a little guilty about hurting him— after all he did seem to think we had some kind of special relationship—she firmly told me I wasn't responsible for his feelings. Walter was definitely getting creepy and today was the last time I planned on seeing him.

We arranged to meet at noon in the deli on the square. I arrived first and took a booth. There was a woman seated in the back of the café. She was wearing dark glasses and a scarf over her head. I thought she looked familiar but couldn't place her. She got up as if to come over to where I was sitting. Then she abruptly turned and went towards the back where the restrooms were. A minute later Walter sat down.

If I meet someone for a meal, I hate it when they sit next to me, especially if we sit in a booth. I feel trapped. I like to talk across the table where I can see their face. I excused myself. "Would you order the salad for me?"

I checked the restroom, but the woman was gone. When I returned to the table, I made sure I was sitting opposite Walter.

"You left in a hurry last night. I wanted to take you to dinner but it seemed you had other plans"

"I did."

"They weren't with the policeman, were they?"

I dropped my eyes modestly. "Yes, they were."

Walter sounded devastated. "But how could you not tell me you were dating someone else?"

Forget Sylvia's advice, lying works so much better. "Sam and I had broken up when I went out with you. But then he came to the show and..." I shrugged my shoulders.

"So you're seeing each other again? Is it serious?"

I nodded and said it was definitely getting that way.

"I really thought we had something, Kate."

"It wasn't working for me, Walter. When I saw Sam again I decided to give it another chance."

"We can we still go out occasionally, can't we?"

I found the more you lie the easier it becomes. "No, that wouldn't work. Sam's the possessive kind."

Walter heaved a big sigh. "I guess I'll have to worship you from afar. But remember, if it doesn't work out..."

"You'll be the first to know."

And with that, I felt as if an enormous weight had been lifted from my shoulders. I almost danced out of the deli. The woman was waiting across the street. I started to walk toward her, but she disappeared around the corner.

When I opened the evening paper it got even better. Our local theater critic had written a long and fulsome review, but the only part that registered said,

"For someone with no lines to deliver, Kate Conley made quite an impact as the slutty maid. She was truly hilarious."

Fame may be fleeting, but it's fun while it lasts.

Chapter 22

I wasn't rid of Walter completely. He had started to hang around the theater. I don't know how he wormed his way into the group because nobody seemed to like him. He was always underfoot, offering to help.

I still had to keep up my façade of a relationship with Sam, but Walter wasn't the brightest. I answered his eager questions as to where I was going with a mysterious smile and that seemed enough to keep him at bay. My one concern was that he would say something to Sam, which would be more than embarrassing, but I decided I'd deal with that issue when or if it arose.

Sam's presence at our opening night surprised me. I don't think of policemen as theatergoers. The only comment he made after dropping Doris off at Frank's place was, "You were very funny as the maid. I enjoyed the show." At least he didn't say slutty maid, but given our history, I felt it was implied.

Frank told me Doris was cooking and cleaning for him. "She's going a little stir crazy, but the house never looked so good."

Frank lived in a neat, little brick ranch on Frontage Road facing I-74. Every time I'd been there it was immaculate with not an item out of place. He also had a large vegetable garden, and it was to this that Doris was applying most of her energy.

"I grow 'em and give away what I can't use, but Doris is making all kinds of preserves and canned stuff. She found my wife's canning supplies in the basement and she's making apple butter right now. I'll bring some in for everyone. There's too much for me to use up."

Sure enough, Frank came to the Friday show loaded down with jars of apple butter and tomatoes. He also brought a couple of apple pies for the green room. I cringed when I saw Walter tagging along behind him carrying a cardboard box full of goodies.

"Look who I ran into on the parking lot. Put the jars on that table over there. Here, take one with you for your help."

He thrust a jar into Walter's hand and disappeared into the wings.

Walter stared at the label then asked, "Are you and the detective still dating?"

Sylvia gasped. "You're dating that hunk of a policeman? Is that why you disappeared opening night? I have to hear all about this." And she pulled me towards the women's dressing room.

I said a hurried goodbye to Walter and hoped someone else would get rid of him. No worries, Sebastian ran a tight ship and only cast and crew were allowed backstage during the show.

The Friday and Saturday shows came and went. Again we got standing ovations. I got to the theater in plenty of time for the Sunday matinee. Stephen was in a big snit because Margaret hadn't turned up.

"She was going to come in early to press the costumes, but she's not here yet, and she's not answering her phone. I'd better start on them or there won't be time to get them done before curtain up."

He grabbed an armful of the most creased and hurried off to the backstage area that he and Margaret had set up as their work space.

I got into costume and started applying makeup. Stephen came in with the newly ironed clothes.

"Kate, you can't wear that apron; it's too grubby. Let me do your hair and I'll look in the basement storage for another. We have two or three more down there."

By this time, backstage was humming with the crew running around checking props and furniture placement, cueing up the sound and resetting lights.

I waited for Stephen to come back with my apron, but he was being pulled in a dozen different directions. I decided to get it myself. Frank stopped me.

"I'll get it for you. I know where Margaret keeps them."

He opened the basement door. "Don't come down the stairs on those heels. They're too steep. You don't want to break your neck."

He leaned forward to switch on the light over the staircase. "I keep meaning to move this. It's in the wrong place. It needs to be closer to the side of the door." The light came on illuminating the stairs. I heard a sound like a cat mewling. Frank went clattering down the stairs.

"Kate, call for an ambulance, right now."

I looked down. There, in a crumpled heap at the bottom of the stairs, was Margaret.

Chapter 23

Frank rode with her to the hospital. The rest of us had to stay and do the show. Stephen was devastated. "I should have known something was wrong. Margaret's never late."

We got through the matinee performance. As cold as it sounds, once the curtain went up we all fell into the same rhythm, felt the same exhilaration.

The reaction came when the show was over. The cast and crew were subdued. There was no joking or laughing about blown lines or audience reaction. Our little ASM had tears trickling down her cheeks as she reset the props table. Sebastian told everyone he would notify them as soon as we found out how Margaret was. Stephen and I were going to the hospital. Sebastian was going back to my house with Enid.

I asked Stephen if she had any family we should call.

"No, she lives alone except for her cat. The theater is her life."

At the hospital, Frank went to check on Margaret and then met us in the waiting room. "She's got a broken leg and a concussion. We can go in to see her but she's pretty doped up."

Margaret lay on her back in the hospital bed. Her right leg was in a cast and a dark bruise ran from the bandage on her head, down the side of her face. Her eyes were closed and tubes snaked from the bags of fluid on a stand next to the bed to the needles taped in her arm.

Frank took her hand gently. "I'm so sorry. I should have moved that light switch and put in another hand rail long ago."

"Not your fault." Her speech was slurred.

I leaned forward over the bed. "Margaret, this is Kate. How did you fall?"

She opened her eyes. "Can't remember..."

She was drifting back into unconsciousness, "...fell...so cold...."

She closed her eyes as the nurse came in, "Sorry, you'll all have to leave now. Visiting hours are over."

Margaret opened her eyes again. She was struggling to say something. I leaned in closer. She whispered in my ear. "Louis."

I looked over at Stephen.

"It's her cat. Don't worry, Margaret. We'll take care of Louis."

"I should have known something was wrong."

We were standing in the hospital corridor outside Margaret's room trying to soothe a distraught Stephen. Around us, people were ebbing and flowing. Frank stepped to one side as a cart came perilously close to running into him.

"Stephen, you can't blame yourself. It was an accident. You couldn't have known."

"But I was angry because I thought she was late and hadn't bothered to call, and all the time she was lying at the foot of the stairs with a broken leg."

"And I should have fixed that light switch weeks ago." Frank's face was grim. "I knew it was dangerous but I kept putting it off because there was always something else to do."

We slowly walked out to the parking lot. I turned to Stephen. "We'll come see her tomorrow. She'll be more coherent then. Who's going to take care of her cat?"

"I will; I've got her keys."

"No way, Stephen. I'll do it."

Frank was ready to argue that it was his responsibility, but I jumped in. "Frank, you've got your hands full taking care of Doris, and I live the closest to Margaret's place anyway."

Earlier that week, I'd told Stephen about Doris' latest scare. He'd apologized for keeping her location secret, but said she was adamant that nobody should know where she was.

"Stephen, give me Margaret's keys. She's only a few blocks from me. You don't even live in Shelbyville."

He reluctantly handed them over and gave me her address.

"Why don't you and Frank go back to the house and let Sebastian and the others know how she is. I'll run over and take care of Louis."

Margaret lived in a red brick, three-story apartment building a couple of blocks behind the hospital. I decided it would be easier to leave my car in the hospital parking lot and walk. I was about a block away when I heard cautious footsteps behind me. They seemed to be keeping pace with mine. When I slowed, so did they. I tried walking a little faster. Sure enough, the footsteps sped up too.

I took a short cut through the alley that ran down the side of Margaret's building. The sun had moved around, leaving pools of darkness in its wake.

About half-way to the end, it occurred to me that walking down a dark, deserted alley when being followed probably wasn't the smartest thing to do. I started hurrying. Whoever was following me quickened their pace too. I turned and looked back. There was a flicker of movement as someone ducked behind a piece of fencing. My heart was pounding, but I made myself walk casually through the rest of the alley to the cross street. As soon as I rounded the corner, I sprinted to the entrance of the apartment building. There was a deep porch in front of the entry door. I squeezed into a corner and waited, slightly winded, trying to slow my breathing.

The footsteps came closer. They slowed, and whoever it was turned and came up the shallow, front steps. She saw me crouched in the corner. For a moment, we stared at each other. Then she turned, ran down the steps and into the street. I didn't follow. I didn't need to, because now I knew who she was and why she was stalking me.

Chapter 24

Frank and I went back to the hospital the next day. I wanted to let Margaret know we were taking good care of Louis.

She was lying in bed and obviously in pain so I decided to make this a short visit.

"Margaret, do you remember your accident?"

"Only parts of it."

"Can you tell us about it?"

Margaret frowned as she tried to concentrate. "I remember being at the theater by myself. I went in early because I wanted to press the costumes before anyone else arrived."

"So you were alone?"

"Yes, but it was strange..." she broke off, thinking hard. "I opened the door with my key and went through the lobby to backstage. I walked towards the dressing rooms to check the costumes. The light was on in the basement so I went over to switch it off. We're always real careful of the lights because we have to keep the electric bill down. Stephen and I were the last ones out of there Saturday night and I was sure we'd checked them but we must have forgotten."

She leaned back against the pillows, her face almost as white as the starched cotton. She reached for the water on the bedside table, but Frank had already picked it up. He held the plastic straw to her lips and we waited while she drank thirstily.

She took a breath and went on, "Anyway, as I said, I went to switch it off. You know how it's kind of hard to get to."

"Yeah, I fixed that first thing this morning," Frank muttered.

"Well, I remember leaning around the door and then I woke up here."

"And you don't remember falling?"

"I don't remember anything."

Margaret's accident bothered me. Something she said, some small detail she mentioned was wrong. But, try as I might, I couldn't recall what it was. I wondered if I should call Sam. I hadn't seen or heard from him since the night we picked Doris up in Danville. But what could I say? That I had this niggling feeling in the back of my mind? I decided to let it be. In the meantime, I would run over to Margaret's place and take care of her cat.

Louis was happy to see me. I spent some time playing with him until he finally crashed on the couch, sated with food and his obviously unaccustomed exercise session. He was the fattest cat I'd ever seen.

After promising to come back that evening and play some more, I gave him one more belly rub and left him to snooze. I had exited the apartment and was carefully locking the door behind me, when I almost collided with someone leaving the apartment opposite. It was a tight space with just two doors on the small landing. We turned at the exact same moment.

It was my stalker.

She looked at me, dropped her eyes and made as if to go down the stairs.

I stopped her. "Wait. Why are you following me?"

"I could ask you the same thing"

"I'm feeding your neighbor's cat while she's in the hospital. What are you doing here?"

She stood for a moment then re-opened her door. "You'd better come in."

The apartment I went into was smaller and shabbier than Margaret's. Someone had tried to brighten it up with posters on the walls. I recognized some from the gift shop at the museum. The furniture was well worn and there were a few stains on the rug, but there were plants and colorful cushions scattered around so the overall effect was cheerful.

I looked at her. The last time I had really seen her was at the museum where we'd both volunteered. Since then she'd changed considerably. Instead of the well groomed, conservatively dressed matron I remembered, she had changed into a younger, more attractive woman with somewhat wild curly hair worn long and loose instead of in the sleek chignon she had favored. Rather than tailored double knit suits, she now wore jeans and a bright sweater.

It was Pamela Moore, Walter's ex-wife.

I took a deep breath. This could be awkward. "Why did you run away from me last night?"

"I don't know. I was following you because I wanted to talk to you, and then you disappeared. When you reappeared in front of my apartment building, I panicked because I didn't want you to find out this was where I lived." She waved an arm in the general direction of the living room and kitchen combination. "It's not exactly what I was used to."

She could say that again. Her parents had owned a beautiful house on a hill overlooking the town. I had never been inside, but I'd loved the red brick exterior and the white columns holding up the two-story porch. It looked like a southern plantation transplanted to the mid-west. I was told she'd had inherited it, along with a substantial sum of money when her parents passed away within two weeks of each other.

She went behind the counter, took down a couple of mugs from the cabinet next to the stove and filled the kettle with water. "You still drink tea, don't you?"

I took a deep breath. "Pamela, I know what you want to say. I've been out, dated, whatever you want to call it, with Walter exactly twice. He spent most of the time talking about you and how devastated he was about the divorce. I have absolutely no intention of seeing him again. Trust me. I'm no threat to you."

I wanted to add that no woman in her right mind could possibly be the slightest bit interested in such a complete and utter bore, but decided against it.

"You think I want to reconcile with Walter?" She gave a bitter laugh. "God knows, it took me long enough to leave him."

I was puzzled. "Then why follow me?"

"I wanted to warn you."

"Warn me?"

"About Walter; he's not what he seems."

Hadn't Sam said that exact same thing?

"You were kind to me when we were on the museum board together and I didn't..." She broke off as the kettle started whistling.

She got up and made the tea. Coming back, she handed me my mug and went on, "When my parents died, they left everything to me. My father had always handled the money and my mom stayed home and took care of the house. I don't think she even knew how to write a check. So when Walter and I married it seemed natural for him to take over."

Pamela was the only child of elderly parents. She had been a year behind me in school, so I didn't know her well. I remembered her as being shy and overly protected by her mother.

"When did you two divorce and why are you living in a place like this? I'm sorry that was rude…"

"Don't apologize—I know it's a dump, but it's all I can afford."

"But surely…" I wanted to say that she must have had some kind of divorce settlement but she forestalled me.

"When Walter and I divorced, there was no money left. He had run through everything I had. I let him have the house because he had mortgaged it to the hilt and I could never afford the payments."

"But he's a dentist. I know he has a thriving practice." Ellie and Jack were among his patients.

"All I know is one day we had money and the next we were broke. He never told me where the money went and, after a time, I was too scared to ask."

She sat in the shabby armchair and slowly sipped her tea. Just as I was about to break the silence and ask another question she said, "Walter can be very manipulative and I didn't want you to be fooled into marrying him like I was. I met him right after my parents died. He wined and dined me, bought me gifts, and told me he was madly in love with me. Like a fool, I believed him. He seemed sweet and caring at first, but he's a cold, cruel man and I lived in fear of him for many years. If it hadn't been for that policewoman, the last time he put me in the hospital…"

I was totally shocked. "Pamela, I'm so sorry; I had no idea…"

She held up her hand to silence me. "It's all right. I'm free of him. I don't care about the money. It's enough that I got away. I tried to follow you to warn you about Walter, but every time I got the courage to approach you, he seemed to turn up."

She dropped her head and spoke so quietly I had to strain to hear her. "The first time he hit me was when I made the mistake of asking him how we had become short of money. He lost his temper and punched me so hard I fell into the fireplace, hit my head and passed out. He cried, said he was sorry, and promised it would never happen again. So I stayed. The beatings became worse and I ended up in the emergency room with broken ribs and a couple of black eyes. After that, I was terrified of saying anything that would set him off. The last time he put me in the hospital, the staff called the police. I was too scared to tell them what happened. I said I'd fallen down the stairs. The policewoman who questioned me tucked the phone number of a women's shelter in my pocket and whispered that I should call them. Walter always checked the phone's directory when he came home, to see who had called that day. I waited until he left for the office then went to a neighbor's house and asked if I could use hers. I told her my phone was out of order. Someone from the shelter called me back and told me where to wait. They came within an hour and picked me up."

She was spilling her tea. I took the mug out of her shaking hands and put it on the counter. "How long were you in the shelter?"

"About three months. The policewoman from the hospital came to see me and brought another policeman with her. They helped me with the paperwork for a restraining order against Walter. They both wanted me to file assault charges against him, but I was too scared. The shelter put me in touch with a free legal office and I filed for divorce."

Her eyes filled with tears. "Please, Kate, don't tell Walter where I live, or that we've talked."

I held her hands in mine. "Don't worry, Pamela. I'm through with Walter. He'll never know we met."

I had one more question, "Which officer came to the shelter to interview you?"

"He was older with gray hair. I think his name was Williams or maybe Williamson."

Now I knew why Sam was so hostile to Walter, and why Walter disappeared every time he saw him.

Chapter 25

To my surprise, Sam called as I was leaving Margaret's building. I hadn't heard from him since the night we picked Doris up in Danville.

"Kate, do you mind if I stop by your apartment? I have a couple of things I need to go over with you."

It was lunchtime when he arrived. Frank had turned up on his way to the library, with two large quiches and an apple pie.

"Doris is still cooking. I'm going to put on twenty pounds unless I find something else for her to do."

I set the table in the kitchen for the three of us. I was hungry and Frank was working the late shift. Sam could eat or not as he chose.

There was a knock at the kitchen door. Sam had parked in the alley and come up the back stairs.

"The outside door downstairs was unlocked."

He did not look pleased. I was certain it had been locked when I'd taken Digger out that morning, and I was careful to lock it behind me. Maybe I should ask Mrs. Turner to check her log?

"I stopped by the hospital and talked to Mrs. Adams. She can't seem to remember anything about the accident, but I have some concerns."

I put the quiche on the table along with a salad, and turned on the coffee-maker.

"Can you and Frank go over again how you found her?"

I looked at Frank and he nodded for me to go ahead. "We had no reason to go to the basement, except I needed a clean apron and Margaret wasn't there to get it. She's the costumer, and she's always on time, and never misses a show," I added, in case Sam didn't understand how unusual it was that Margaret wasn't there. "I started to go down for it, but Frank stopped me. He said my heels were too high and the stairs were too steep, so he would get the apron."

Frank picked up the narrative. "I leaned around to switch on the light and I heard something. I looked down and saw Margaret at the foot of the stairs. I told Kate to call for an ambulance. You know the rest."

Sam frowned. I put a large piece of quiche on a plate and handed it to him. He took it and absently started eating, but I could see his mind was elsewhere. He finished his quiche in two large bites and stood up to go.

Frank got ready too. "I'm off. See you later, Kate."

Sam made as if to follow him out. I stopped him. "Sam, do you have a minute? I need to talk to you about something."

He turned back from the door.

"Sam, I felt that you had a lot of..." I searched for the right word, but all I could come up with was hostility. It would have to do, "hostility towards Walter Moore. When you told me I should be more careful about the men I date, I was angry because..." I broke off.

"You thought I was interfering?"

"No...."

"Then...?"

"It's just that you made it sound as if I were too stupid to figure anything out for myself... Anyway, I know you were trying to warn me about him, and I want to apologize for being rude to you."

There, I'd got it out.

"So what made you change your mind about Moore?"

"I talked to his ex-wife. I know about the restraining order. But I'd decided to drop Walter after the first date."

"Because?"

"Because he was so totally boring, I didn't care if I ever saw him again. But he kept calling and hanging around."

Sam was trying not to smile. "How did you get rid of him?"

"He saw us leave together that night at the theater and got the mistaken idea that we were dating. When he asked me if that's why I wasn't going to see him anymore, I said yes, because it was an easy way of getting rid of him."

"So Walter Moore thinks we're a couple?"

"I was worried he might say something to you, but after talking to his ex-wife, I now know he was avoiding you."

"You don't need to apologize, Kate. I was out of line. You would have figured him out without my help. That's why I sent the flowers."

I was flabbergasted. "You sent me the roses?"

"To…you know...say I was sorry…I've got to go." His ears were red and he couldn't get out of the door fast enough.

I stood there with my mouth hanging open. Sam sent me the roses? We were barely civil to each other.

Chapter 26

I was enjoying a lazy day. Tonight would be the
closing performance of the play and we had a big backstage party planned for after the curtain came down for
the last time. I put the kettle on for tea and was reaching
for my mug when Digger pushed at my leg with his
cold nose. He needed to go out.

After checking that Rose and Enid's cat wasn't
around, I took him down the back stairs. He went
straight to his favorite tree then started wandering
aimlessly around the yard following one scent after
another. I called him to heel and we went back up the
stairs. About half way up, he started whining. I looked
around but the cat was nowhere in sight.

"Come on, Digger; you're safe. Petey's in his own
apartment."

I patted him on the head and he followed me to the
kitchen door. As I opened it, he shot in ahead of me and
immediately disappeared. As I turned to lock the door,
it burst open, pinning me against the wall.

"Where is she?"

The man from the airport grabbed me and pushed
my head against the hard surface of the refrigerator. His
fingers dug viciously into my neck.

"The old lady—what have you done with her?"

For one moment, I was amazingly calm. It was like
when your car hits a patch of ice and starts spinning
out. Time stops and everything happens in slow motion.
The car seems to move in slow concentric circles

forever, but you know eventually the collision will come.

Then the panic hit. I tried to bite the hand clutching my throat. He pushed my head away contemptuously. I reached up and ripped his sunglasses off his face. His eyes were dark, flat, with pinpoint pupils. I jabbed them with my nails. He growled, stepped back, and punched me in the gut. I fell forward, almost vomiting. He grabbed me by the front of my shirt. I felt the buttons pop. Then my forgotten tea kettle started its shrill whistling. It startled him and his grip loosened as he turned towards the noise. I pulled away and ran into the hallway. He came after me and caught me by my hair, yanking it viciously.

"Tell me where she is or you'll be sorry."

"I don't know—I swear. She left in the middle of the night a few weeks ago and nobody's seen or heard from her since."

"You're lying."

As he dragged me down the hallway, I could still hear the shriek of the boiling kettle. If I could get to it maybe I could throw it at him. But he was pulling me the other way towards the front door. That's when Digger saved me. He had his tail sticking out of the coat closet where he was hiding and the kidnapper stepped on it. Digger howled and jumped into the man's legs, startling him. He lost his footing and let go of my hair. I pulled away and ran for the door. The man lunged for me, but Digger managed to get tangled up in his legs again. That gave me enough time to get out.

I flew down the stairs, his footsteps pounding after me. Rose and Enid's door opened as he ran past. Rose stepped out and hit him squarely on the back of the head with a large iron skillet.

"Pole-axed the bastard," she declared triumphantly.

He collapsed into the back of me, throwing me into the wall at the foot of the stairs. My head connected with the oak hallstand. My attacker crumpled to the floor. I heard hammering on the front door and passed out.

I awakened to someone shining a light in my eyes. The hallway seemed full of people. I was lying on the floor. My attacker had disappeared. The front door was open and there was a gurney to my right. I tried to sit up but the EMT with the light gently pushed me back down.

"Take it easy, ma'am. We're still checking you out."

The "we" included the woman doing something with what looked like a blood pressure cuff around my arm.

"Where's the man who was chasing me?"

"He's on his way to the lockup." That was a familiar voice.

"Sam?"

I looked around. Four anxious pairs of eyes stared down at me. They belonged to Enid, Rose, Sam and Martha. Digger watched the scene anxiously from the half landing, too intimidated by the chance of running into Petey to descend any further.

Sam knelt down at my side. "You're going to be all right, Kate. The ambulance is outside. We'll have you at the hospital in a few minutes."

I shook off the cuff wrapped around my arm and struggled to a sitting position. "I'm not going to the hospital. I have a show to do." I may have been a novice actor but one thing I knew was the show must go on. It was going on with me, not some understudy, playing the slutty maid.

There was a commotion at the front door. Doris rushed in with Frank close behind, carrying her old suitcase and shabby purse.

"Now that the man's been caught, I can come home."

She saw me on the floor with Sam next to me, "What happened? Frank just said the man was in custody. Nobody told me Kate was hurt."

Frank gave me an apologetic look. "When Enid called and said the attacker had been arrested, there was no stopping Doris. I've never seen anyone pack so fast."

"Help me up, Frank." I held out my hand and he hauled me to my feet.

As I made my unsteady way towards the stairs, Sam was right behind me. I felt his supporting arm as he kept saying, "Don't be foolish, Kate; you need to go to the emergency room."

I ignored him.

Chapter 27

I was resting on my couch, propped up on pillows, with a blanket tucked tightly around my legs. Doris was in the kitchen making my long delayed cup of tea.

She popped her head around the door. "The kettle's a goner, burnt to a crisp. I'll get a new one when I go to the store."

She was back a few minutes later, carrying my tea. "Are you sure you'll be well enough to do the show?"

"My throat hurts, my head is sore and my stomach aches where that man punched me. But I don't have any lines and I can cover the bruises on my head and neck with makeup. I'm not missing our last performance."

Doris set her lips and didn't argue. I was thankful for that small mercy. I had gone through a few intense minutes with Sam urging me to go to the hospital. He only stopped when I lay back on my pillows, closed my eyes and pretended to feel faint.

Digger slunk into the room and put a paw up on the couch. He was overwhelmed by all the praise and attention he'd received when I told everyone about his part in my escape from the attacker.

Sam, in particular, seemed ecstatic. "I told you he would be protection for you."

I hadn't mentioned that Digger had been hiding in the closet like the craven coward he was. If Sam and Martha wanted to deem him a hero, I'd let them. After all, he had tripped the man which allowed me to escape.

Doris was thrilled to finally be able to see the finished production. "Frank told me you were a big hit. I can't wait to see the show."

Closing night was wonderful. We got so many standing ovations that Sebastian had to ring down the curtain and tell the audience to go home, which got another standing ovation.

And we had a great party in the green room.

The only down side was that Sam wasn't there. He and Martha left soon after Doris came home, so I never had a chance to thank him for the flowers.

The next morning, Doris and I were having a leisurely breakfast before going in to the theater to help break down the set. The adrenaline rush of the previous evening had dissipated. Sebastian told me I should stay home and rest. He was probably right. Everything was hurting, from the top of my head where the kidnapper had grabbed me by the hair, to the bruises on my neck which were turning multiple shades of purple and yellow. My abdomen ached as if I'd been run over by a truck—not that I knew how that felt—just that it was painful.

"Kate, are you sure you're up to working today?" Doris asked anxiously.

"I don't think I'll be lifting anything heavy, but I know there's something I can do."

Since Margaret was still in the hospital, Doris would be at the theater all day working on costume storage. I wasn't ready to stay home by myself. My brain told me I was safe. The kidnapper was in jail, or rather in a hospital ward, handcuffed to a bed and surrounded by guards, unconscious and likely to stay that way for a while. But the rest of me panicked every time I heard a door open. Doris was now taking Digger out for his daily constitutionals. I would recover, but for now I went with my gut, my still aching gut, which told me I needed to be around people, not alone.

Frank insisted on driving us to the theater. He also took Margaret's keys from me and fed Louis, for which I was profoundly grateful. I didn't have the energy to climb up three flights of stairs.

The next few hours were frantically busy, tearing down and storing the flats. I let the more fit members of the group lift the heavy scenery and furniture. I sorted props into categories and supervised repacking the set decorations we had borrowed so they would be labeled, and ready for their owners to pick up.

Stephen and Doris collected the costumes. They had a large rolling rack, and were sorting those that needed dry cleaning from those that were going to be washed or just pressed and stored. One of our patrons owned a dry cleaning store and had generously donated cleaning costs.

Doris was her usual dynamo self. Sebastian had to stop her from carrying the finished costumes down to the basement storage. "Let's sort the costumes up here and Stephen will carry them down the stairs. We don't want any more accidents."

I sat in an old armchair opposite the basement door trying to keep out of everyone's way. My limited store of energy was gone and I ached all over. Sylvia offered to take me home, but I wanted to stay until Doris was ready to leave. I still didn't want to be home by myself.

I leaned back in the chair and briefly closed my eyes.

A voice at my right ear said, "Kate, are you almost finished here?"

I turned and looked. It was the last person I wanted to see. I felt like punching his stupid face but didn't have the energy. Instead I said, "What do you want, Walter?"

"I noticed all the cars outside, and took a chance you'd be here. I don't see the detective boyfriend anywhere about—maybe we could grab an early dinner."

I was through being nice to him. "I told you, I'm not ever going out with you again. Stop bothering me. If you need me to make it any plainer, I'll have the detective boyfriend explain it to you. Maybe he can make you understand."

There was no reply. I looked at him. His face had lost all color and he was backing away from me. Stephen had just come up from the basement and Doris was handing him more costumes. Sylvia was walking toward me with a hot cup of tea in her hand. They froze in some kind of tableau watching him.

"You're...you're..." he started to say, and then he turned and almost ran out of the theater.

"That was strange. What did you say to him?"

"Nothing—I just told him to stop bothering me."

"Well, it worked," said Doris. "Doesn't look as if you'll be hearing from him any time soon."

If only I'd realized it was that easy.

The next morning, I dragged my aching body out of bed and into the kitchen for a reviving cup of tea.

"How's my little sweetheart this morning? Are you ready for a lovely breakfast?"

I stopped, amazed. Doris was never that sentimental. Then I realized she was talking to Digger, not me. He was sitting near the back door, gazing up at her with adoring eyes.

She saw me. "The water's on for tea. I'm going to fix you a good breakfast. Then I need more food for Digger. I'll go to the store as soon as we eat. You stay here and rest."

By the time Doris had fed Digger and me, her list had grown. Digger needed canned food, treats to reward him when he did something right, dog biscuits for his teeth, plus some chew toys and a Frisbee.

"That's too much for you to carry home, Doris. I don't feel up to shopping, but I'll drive you to the store and wait in the car."

I parked at the end of the row and watched Doris disappear into the market. I leaned back against the seat and closed my eyes. Even the short trip to the store had been an effort. I was almost asleep, when I heard a familiar voice. My eyes shot open.

"Just one more stop for the wine, and we have everything for a great dinner."

Another voice—one I didn't recognize—answered, "I'll have it ready when you get home. Call me when you're leaving the station."

I scooted down in the seat until my nose was level with the bottom of the window and took a cautious peek. It was Sam. His SUV was parked one slot over from mine. Standing next to him, helping him unload the groceries, was a stunningly beautiful woman, not much older than Ellie. She had a mass of auburn hair and from the way they were leaning toward each other and laughing, they seemed to be old friends. Sam put his arms around her. "I'm so glad you're here."

No, definitely more than friends, I decided. I sank deeper in my seat. I had left the house in a pair of old baggy sweat pants and a faded tee-shirt. My hair was scraped back into a rubber band, and I didn't have on a scrap of makeup.

My next car, I told myself as Sam and his *inamorata* drove away without a glance in my direction, was going to have tinted windows—dark tinted windows.

Chapter 28

I had a hard time sleeping that night. My head hurt where the kidnapper had grabbed me by the hair, my throat was still sore, and my stomach muscles screamed every time I tossed and turned in the bed. Everything was going round and around in my head. Some things I was beginning to figure out, others totally eluded me.

The past few months had flown by. I had gone from my safe, easy life with Jack to total chaos. I picked up the pieces and moved on to a new life, which was turning out to be much more fun than the old one, apart from a few minor glitches, such as being attacked by a crazed would-be kidnapper.

But there were many unanswered questions. Why had Jack been in my apartment that night? He professed to not remember. The head injury had supposedly wiped out his memory of that evening. Even if that were true—which I didn't believe—there had to be a reason for him coming to the house. Things were still strained between Ellie and me. I was sure she felt I was involved in some way.

Digger came into my room. Instead of jumping on the bed and putting his head on the pillow next to mine, he started whining. Surely he didn't want out? Yes, he did. He was doing his little bathroom dance. Doris was snoring in the next room.

I threw on some sweats over my pajamas and quietly left through the kitchen door, carefully locking it behind me. Digger rushed down the stairs, pushed open the outside door with his nose and flew out into the yard. After lifting his leg against his favorite tree, he started wandering around, following one interesting scent after another. I called him to heel, put him back on the leash and started towards the door. I had my hand on the handle, ready to open it, when I heard someone coming down the stairs.

We hadn't seen or heard our upstairs neighbor since the night of my disastrous dinner date with Walter. Sam had asked us to let the police department know when he came back, but we'd decided he must have moved out. I hid in the shadow by the side of the outside door and waited. As the hooded figure went past, Digger whined and pulled the leash out of my hand. Whoever it was went running across the yard, with Digger in hot pursuit, and me chasing Digger.

"Wait!" I yelled, "I just want to talk to you."

The person put on a burst of speed, with Digger keeping pace and me lagging behind. I would have lost him, but Digger saved the day again. As he flew across the yard to the alley, the runner stepped into one of Digger's holes and went sprawling across the grass. A black back-pack flew from his hand. I tripped over it, and landed on top of the body. The hood slipped back, exposing a mass of blonde hair. It was the last person I expected to see—Tiffany, my ex-husband's trophy wife.

She tried to struggle out from under me, but I held fast. Now the pieces of the puzzle were starting to come together.

"Isn't it a little late to be visiting your boyfriend?"

"That's nothing to do with you. I have every right to be here"

"Now I know what Jack was doing the night he was attacked. Checking up on you, right? What else happened? Did your lover and my ex-husband get into a fight?"

She was silent.

I sat firm. "I'm not letting you go until I get answers. I get why he was in the house, but why in my apartment?"

"You think you know it all, but you don't know anything," she spat at me.

She tried to struggle up again and hit my aching gut with her elbow. I grabbed a handful of her hair and held on.

"You stupid bitch, let go of me." She started screaming and cursing. I saw her elbow come towards me again so I leaned forward and ground her face into the dirt, which sent her into a further frenzy as she tried to spit out the clumps of grass and mud she'd inhaled.

I saw flashing lights and a patrol car pull up behind us. A police officer jumped out, weapon drawn. An unmarked car racketed into the alley behind him. It was Sam and Martha. True to her word, the ever vigilant Mrs. Turner had called the police.

Tiffany started screaming, "Arrest her! She attacked me."

Sam walked over and hauled me to my feet. Tiffany fell silent when she saw him. Martha carefully picked up the dropped back-pack and put it into a plastic evidence bag. The patrol officer placed the bag in the trunk of his car. Tiffany was escorted into the back seat. The officer pulled away, leaving me with Sam and Martha.

An angry Sam took me to one side. "What the hell are you doing fighting with Tiffany in the back yard, in the middle of the night? You've barely recovered from the last incident."

He was right. Now the adrenaline was ebbing, I started to feel my aches and bruises again.

"I was out with Digger and I heard Tiffany coming down from the upstairs tenant's apartment. She fell in one of Digger's holes. I was trying to find out what she was doing here."

"Did you ever think of calling and letting me handle it?"

"It just happened, Sam. Digger started chasing her. When she fell, I tripped over her."

A pulse in his jaw started throbbing. "I'll stop by when I can. Try to be home."

Chapter 29

"Why don't we try color?"

I was sitting in front of the mirror at the beauty shop with Stephen hovering in the background, lifting strands of my hair. He had wanted to try a different color on my hair for the last couple of years, but I had always resisted.

"We could go a couple of shades lighter with some highlights and maybe lowlights too." He ran his fingers over my scalp. I winced.

"Sorry, I forgot it's still sore. I'll be more careful. Why don't I give you a different cut?"

I looked at his spiked blond hair with the blue highlights. "Nothing too, um...bright or weird, all right?"

I was ready for something new. This had nothing to do with seeing Sam with his girlfriend. It was something I had planned to do as soon as the show ended its run and I no longer needed my "big hair" look.

"Put yourself in my hands. You'll love the result."

And I did. I was in the chair for over two hours, but it was worth every minute.

"Stephen, you're the best. I love the cut. I love the color."

And what I didn't say was, I loved the way I looked, and I loved the way it made me feel. Clothes may make the man, but a new hairstyle and color, plus manicure and pedicure, definitely does wonders for the woman.

Stephen inclined his head as if to acknowledge he was the master. "I'm not going to say I told you so, but I told you so."

When I arrived home, Doris informed me that Sam had stopped in. "He wasn't happy that you weren't here."

Too bad, I thought. Aloud, I said, "Did you tell him to call before coming, next time?"

"I told him I thought you'd be back later."

Sam turned up as Doris and I were sitting down to an early dinner. Doris had slept through the whole incident with Digger and Tiffany the night before. I had just finished filling her in on the details when he knocked on the door.

Doris let him in, sat him down at the table, and before he could utter a single word, slid a large steaming plate of pot roast and gravy under his nose. I filled his coffee cup while a bemused Sam stared at his plate.

He automatically picked up his fork, thought better of it and placed it by the side of the plate. "I stopped by this morning. I expected you to be home."

"Maybe you should call before coming over. It would have saved you a wasted trip."

Sam opened his mouth to say something, thought better of it, and stuffed a healthy portion of Doris' pot roast in his mouth.

Doris refilled my plate and plonked down a large glass of wine next to my place, as if to say *drink it and be nice*. She put the bottle in the center of the table.

"With all that's been happening around here lately, I'd have thought you'd have more sense than to start a fight with someone in your back yard in the middle of the night. Why didn't you call me? Or Martha?" he added hastily.

"Thank you, but may I remind you the kidnapper has been arrested and I no longer need a caretaker? And furthermore," my voice started to rise, "if I hadn't gone outside with Digger, the dog you begged me to take in, you would never have learned there was a connection between Tiffany and the upstairs tenant. I think you should be thanking, not berating me, for doing your job for you."

We glared at each other across the table. Sam dropped his eyes first. He picked up his fork and started eating. Doris took the opportunity to place a basket of hot, buttered biscuits and the honey jar in front of him.

He dribbled a little honey on a couple of biscuits, crammed one in his mouth, followed by a hearty swig of coffee. No doubt about it, the man inhaled food as if he hadn't eaten in a week. He also looked as if he hadn't slept in a week. His shirt was creased, and he must have shaved with one eye shut, because he'd missed more than a few spots. Unlike the rejuvenated Jack, having a young girlfriend seemed to be having an aging effect on Sam.

"What was in the back-pack that Tiffany seemed so anxious to protect?"

He hesitated, "That's evidence. I can't talk about it."

I opened my mouth to argue, but Doris broke in, "I bet that nasty young man and Tiffany are carrying on behind her husband's back. I always told you, Kate, a young girl like that'd get tired of having an old man for a husband."

Sam shook his head. "No, Doris, that's what I thought at first, but I was wrong. We found out last night, he's her brother." He cleared his throat and continued. "Well, half brother, same mother, different fathers. That's why we didn't make the connection."

"Her brother?" I was confused. "Then why was she sneaking around late at night to see him?"

"Her brother was the one who tried to break into your apartment a few weeks ago. He's been staying elsewhere since then. She was at the apartment to pack up his belongings."

"You didn't answer my question. Why does she have to sneak around to see him?"

"Because he was released from the federal penitentiary in Terre Haute six months ago, and Tiffany didn't want her new husband to find out she had a jailbird brother. Unfortunately, she had to call your ex-husband to bail her out, so now he knows. She also wanted you arrested for assault, but he didn't seem too keen on the idea."

He went on, "Your ex-husband has miraculously recovered from his amnesia and decided to come clean—well, partially clean. He told us he was at your apartment that night, because he found out that Tiffany was sneaking off somewhere every Thursday night when he was attending a meeting at church. He followed her to your place. He says he didn't know you lived at that address, and he didn't know the apartment he went into was yours. I think that part is true."

It probably was. Jack was so wrapped up in his new life, with his new hair and new sports car, to say nothing of the new trophy wife, he had little time to wonder what had happened to wife number one. All he knew was I had sold our former home and lived in what Ellie described as the "bad" part of town.

Sam took another honey-covered biscuit and washed it down with the last of his coffee. Doris lifted the wine bottle enquiringly, but he shook his head. She hastily refilled his coffee cup, not wanting to miss a word.

"Anyway, he saw her enter the house and followed her up the back stairs. Your apartment door was open. There was a man going in. She followed him and he followed her. He says the rest is a blank."

"Do you believe him?"

"I believe his story up until he went into your kitchen, but there's more he isn't telling us. There's a lot of tension between them. She was sobbing and trying to hang on to him, but he pushed her away."

"So it was her brother who went into my apartment? Why? And why did Tiffany follow him?"

'The brother's name is Wayne Plekowski. He's got a lengthy record, starting with a liquor store robbery when he was a teenager, and more recently for dealing drugs. Tiffany says he broke in to steal whatever he could find, because he needed money, and she had given him all she could without her husband becoming suspicious. I think it was an easy job for him. As you know, he had a key that fit your lock."

"Which, if I remember, I had to point out to you."

His eyes narrowed, and the familiar flinty look was back. He ignored what I said and continued. "His sister was trying to stop him because if he were caught, with his record, he'd be back in prison for a long time. They seem close. She says that Jack was fine when they left, and that you must be the one who attacked him."

"What does Jack say?"

"He says he doesn't remember anything after going inside the apartment, but he's lying about that."

"Well, it's lucky I have an alibi," I said calmly.

"I didn't tell them about your alibi yet. Tiffany insists she and her brother left right away. But we know from Mrs. Turner's log that the brother left first, and she followed about ten minutes later. I'm saving that for further questioning."

He went on, "We're pretty certain that either Tiffany, or her brother, hit Jack over the head. She stayed behind to clean up. It was a pretty cold thing to do. He could have died if you hadn't come home when you did."

Sam ran a hand over his face. He looked exhausted. "I have to go—there's a lot going on down at the precinct. If you hear any movement upstairs call Martha or me—don't try to handle it yourselves."

"Wait, what about the kidnapper?"

"We can't question him yet. He's still unconscious. When we do, I'll let you know what we find out."

He gave a last lingering look at the biscuits and left by the kitchen door after reminding me to lock it behind him.

Chapter 30

The day after Sam's visit, Doris was watching one of her morning shows on the television in the den. I was in the kitchen filling Digger's empty bowl with food. We'd fed him once that morning, but Doris thought he was too skinny and needed fattening up, so any time I saw the bottom of his bowl I put food in it.

"Kate, come here, quick."

It sounded urgent. I dropped the bag of food and rushed into the room, "What's going on? What do you want?"

She pointed at the television screen, "Look. It's a drug bust, right here in Shelbyville."

Someone was hammering at my front door. I ran to open it and Enid and Rose almost fell through the doorway. "Are you watching television? Something big is going on."

We crowded into the den. A reporter was standing in a light rain, outside City Hall, talking breathlessly into a microphone.

"A major drug ring that originated in Arizona has been broken up right here in Shelbyville. Simultaneous raids took place at a motel in Indianapolis, and a truck stop on the south side of that city. Over twenty people were taken into custody. The raids were carried out by a joint task force from the Shelbyville and Indianapolis police departments, and the U.S. Marshall's office"

The TV station cut to a press conference already in progress. Reporters were shouting questions at a spokesperson from the mayor's office. He was saying,

"...a major drug operation has been shut down. Crystal meth, manufactured in Mexico, was shipped through Arizona and trucked into Indiana. We are confident that we have shut down a major supply route to the Midwest and beyond."

"Can you tell us how many local people were involved?"

"That information will be available later in the day."

"How much of the drug was sold in Shelby County?"

"We don't have exact numbers, but the investigation started last year when crystal meth was discovered in students' lockers at the high school."

There was a noise above our heads, a crash as if something heavy had been dropped, then sound of footsteps, then silence. Doris dived for the phone, but it rang before she could reach it. It was Mrs. Turner.

Doris listened intently, then turned to us. "Mrs. Turner says she saw the upstairs tenant sneaking down the back stairs." She listened some more and turned to us again. "She called the police and they're coming to pick him up."

She hung up. "I have to get off the phone in case she has to use it again."

Then everything happened at once. The phone rang. We heard the crash of a door being flung back on its hinges and pounding feet running up the back stairs. Rose ran for the front door, but before she got to it, we heard the downstairs door crash inward, and more footsteps. They passed our apartment and continued up the stairs. There was a lot of yelling, more doors crashing in, the sound of footsteps overhead, a panicked "Don't shoot...don't shoot," then silence.

"Who wants to call our landlord and tell him the doors need fixing again?" said Rose.

The next day we were glued to the television set. In addition to Enid and Rose, Frank was there. He had stopped in to deliver another bag of dog food on his way back from feeding Louis. Digger had found the bag I'd dropped on the kitchen floor the day before and eaten every scrap of food and about half the paper bag as well. We found him sleeping it off with a distended belly and a blissful smile on his doggy face.

"Wait. They're talking about the brother now." Frank turned up the sound on the remote.

The TV station cut back to the first reporter, "Also arrested yesterday in the same house where police previously arrested a known drug dealer who had attacked one of the tenants, was Wayne Plekowski. Plekowski has been arrested numerous times on drug and burglary charges. He was released from the federal penitentiary in Terre Haute earlier this year. Since his release, he has been living in the house where he was arrested."

A picture of our house flashed up on the screen. I gave it five minutes before Ellie called. I was off by three. The phone rang. I picked it up to hear, "Mom, do you see what went on at your house?"

"Of course, I was here when the raid took place."

"You should never have sold the house. Andrew warned you about living in that part of town."

Doris yelled at me across the room.

"Hold on, Ellie. What did you say, Doris?"

"Listen to this…"

The earnest local anchor was saying, "Plekowski is the brother of Tiffany Conley, wife of a prominent local attorney who's rumored to be running for a seat on the City Council."

"Did you hear that, Ellie? The guy who was arrested is Tiffany's brother. She was here, in his apartment, two nights ago. I ran into her in my backyard when I took the dog out. That puts a whole different slant on what your father was doing in my apartment, doesn't it?"

There was silence, then, "I'll call you back later." And she hung up the phone.

It rang again. "When did you get a dog?"

Chapter 31

Mrs. Turner had so much information to enter into her daily log she had to start a new notebook. She and Doris were on the phone for almost an hour while she took notes on everything that went on during the raid. Our landlord called. I passed him off to Doris. She loved talking on the phone, plus she always had more information than I did.

It was five days before we got the whole story. Sam and Martha came to the apartment. The doors had been repaired—again. Doris baked a cake and had coffee ready. We were both anxious to hear what they had to say.

Sam's face was gray with exhaustion and Martha didn't look much better. They sat and took out their notebooks.

"Well, come on, tell us what happened." Doris was champing at the bit.

Sam kneaded his forehead with both hands, opened his notebook and started.

"We've been working on this drug case for the past year, ever since meth turned up at the high school. We've always had a problem with locally made meth, but it was usually out in the county. It's too easily spotted in the city."

"How?" Doris wanted to know.

"The manufacturing process gives off toxic fumes and stinks up the neighborhood pretty badly. People living around it report to us because they're afraid of an explosion. It can be extremely volatile. And you can spot the users right off."

Before Doris could ask again, he quickly added, "They'll have what is called a meth mouth—lesions, especially around their mouths, a drawn and haggard look, missing teeth—they usually seem at least ten years older than their actual age—they smell as bad as their product."

Martha cleared her throat as if telling him to get to the point. He looked down at his notebook and continued.

"Let's get to the man who tried to kidnap you at the airport, and attacked Kate here in her apartment. He goes by the name of Johnny Dee, though that's not his real name. He's originally from Hawaii. He disappeared from there a few years ago, and has been living in various parts of the Midwest ever since. He's a distant relative of your son's wife. I'm sorry…"

Doris interrupted him, "Let's just get to it. I'm pretty sure I know what you're going to say."

"Within an hour of your leaving their house, either your son or his wife called Dee and had a forty minute conversation with him. They adamantly deny hiring him to kidnap you, or to kill your cousin to stop him being the beneficiary of your estate. Dee tells a different story. He says he was hired to kidnap and kill you, but says he only planned to scare you. He says he didn't kill your cousin and his secretary, but we know he was in Wadesboro at the time of the shooting—we have him on the traffic cams returning to Indianapolis and we found the gun he used hidden in his motel room."

Doris nodded her head, as if to say she knew it all along.

"And we have him dead to rights on the attack on Kate. So he'll be going away for a very long time."

"How much did I go for?"

Sam knew what she meant. "We don't know that part yet. We do know Dee needed money to buy into the meth trade, which is why he was so desperate to find you. As for your son and his wife, they're deeply in debt and were on the point of losing their house."

"And they thought I would be their cash cow?"

"Pretty much."

"And when they couldn't get the money from me, they called this Johnny Dee person?"

"Yes."

Doris was silent for a moment, then, "Why did he have to kill Charlie? He could have just taken me at the airport."

Sam said gently, "But then your cousin would have driven down to Indianapolis to pick you up, and if you weren't there, he would start asking questions. For someone like Dee, it was a loose end he couldn't afford."

She bowed her head and sat silent for a few minutes.

To give her time to recover, I asked about Tiffany's brother. "Was our upstairs tenant involved in the meth deal?"

"No; we're questioning him about the attack on your ex-husband and the break-ins at your apartment."

"Break-ins?"

"We think he was the man who tried to enter your apartment the night you were out with..." he stopped and covered himself with a cough, "when you were out to dinner, as well as breaking in the night your ex-husband was attacked. He's not admitting to anything yet. He's saying he was drunk and mistook your apartment for his. He and his sister deny attacking Jack, but right about now we have officers serving Tiffany with a search warrant for her clothes. Your ex-husband is still sticking to his partial amnesia story. All he admits to is following his wife to your house, and going into the kitchen."

"Does he still say he thinks I attacked him?"

"No. I think he sees the writing on the wall and wants to distance himself from both his new wife Tiffany and his felon brother-in-law."

"And the brother got into my apartment with his own key."

It was a statement, not a question. I still hadn't forgotten, or forgiven, my first circle of hell.

"Yes, which is why we saw no sign of forced entry. Tiffany and Plekowski still say they left together and Jack stayed behind."

"What do you think happened?"

"I think your ex-husband followed his wife here, not knowing this was where you lived. I think Tiffany saw her brother going into your apartment. She followed him—either to stop him or help him. Jack confronted Plekowski because he thought he was Tiffany's lover, and one of them hit Jack over the head with the urn and cracked his skull. That version fits Mrs. Turner's timeline. The brother left first while Tiffany cleaned up, which is why there were no fingerprints on the door or urn. It must have taken her about ten minutes, which matches the time Mrs. Turner documented her leaving."

"So neither of them admits to hitting Jack over the head with my majolica urn?"

"Not yet."

Sam's cell vibrated. He got up and walked out in the hall. We sat in silence until he returned.

"That was the officer in charge of serving the warrant. They've found a pair of Tiffany's sneakers that look as if there's blood in the treads. If it turns out to be your husband's blood…"

"Ex-husband," I said under my breath.

"Then we can prove one of them attacked him. Since she stepped in the blood, they had to have been there when he was lying on the floor bleeding. The question is which one hit him?"

Chapter 32

Two days after Sam's visit, Doris disappeared again. She left a note saying she had some business to take care of, and would I turn the crock pot off at three if she wasn't back by then.

Life was slowly returning to normal. I went back to my library job. The furor about the drug raids slowly died down. I watched for any mention of Tiffany or her brother in the news, and on the day Doris disappeared again, I finally went to visit Ellie and the boys.

Ellie was devastated. She sat next to me on the couch, sobbing. "I don't know what's going on and Dad won't tell me anything. Poor Dad, he wanted to run for a seat on the city council, but after such a messy divorce from you, and now this thing with Tiffany, he doesn't think he has a chance of being elected."

I rubbed her back the way I used to when she came home from grade school with a problem. "I'm sorry, sweetheart. Your father made some poor choices and he has to take responsibility for them. If he'd been honest with me and told me he wanted a divorce, I would have been hurt—all right, probably furious—but it could have been civilized. Instead, he takes me away for a romantic weekend to celebrate our thirtieth anniversary, and two days later I find him screwing Tiffany on top of the desk I bought him for his fiftieth birthday."

The desk still rankled.

Ellie stopped crying for a moment. She looked at me with such a piteous face, I felt guilty for reminding her of the sordid details of why I had attacked Jack with his golf club.

"But, Mom, he never intended to marry her. He said it was a mid-life crisis. If you hadn't made such a fuss, and gotten it in the papers, it would have just petered out."

"Are you saying all this is my fault? I should have ignored the affair?"

"No, but after all the publicity, he was almost forced into marrying her."

"Ellie," I said quietly, "what if you had walked in on Andrew having sex with his secretary? What would you have done?"

"Andrew would never do such a thing."

"And I never thought your father would either."

For all Ellie's dismissal of Jack's affair with Tiffany as a mid-life crisis—I wasn't buying it. Jack had been totally obsessed with his new life style—the hair plugs, the red sports car, the blonde bimbo. I had always thought of Jack as a good solid man, ethical and honest. How could I have not seen how shallow and vain he was? Why had I tried so hard to make it seem as if our marriage were perfect? Looking back, it had been downright boring. And had I learned anything from my mistakes? So far I'd had a drunken one night stand with Sam, and a couple of dates with a spousal abuser. And I hadn't yet found the courage to tell my family I was divorced—still trying to be the perfect child.

The conversation with Ellie left me angry and unsettled. Doris still wasn't home. I turned off the crock pot and decided to take Digger for a long walk. I calmed down after jogging around the high school track a couple of times, and I was in a better mood when I got back.

Coming in the through the alley, I saw two men around the side of the house. They both had clipboards and were looking up at the house and taking notes. Digger and I walked over to them. "Hi, you want to tell me what you're doing here?"

"Just checking on some things for the real estate company."

"But why?"

"Don't know, lady."

Did that mean the owner was selling the house? In spite of everything that had happened here, I loved my apartment and I loved living with Doris, Rose and Enid. I didn't want to move.

Doris still hadn't returned, so I couldn't discuss it with her. I wondered if I should be concerned. She'd never been away this long by herself, except for the time she'd run away to Phil's place in Lafayette.

Sam turned up as I was about to call and try to track Doris down. I opened my mouth to ask why he was there, when he casually said, "I've found a good home for Digger. It's with a nurse I know who works in the emergency room at Major Hospital. When she heard what a good guard dog he was, she said she would definitely take him."

I exploded. "I don't care who she is or where she works, she's not getting our dog. You can tell her to forget it. We're keeping him."

Sam threw his head back and started laughing. "You should see your face. Martha made a bet with me that you wouldn't let him go. I guess I'll have to break the bad news to Nora."

"You do that."

I walked into the kitchen, leaving Sam to find his own way out, but instead of leaving, he followed me.

"Would you like to know the latest developments?"

I took a deep breath. "I'm still angry with you for even thinking we would give up Digger, but yes, I would like to know what's going on. There's been nothing in the news."

He sat down at the table. "We confronted Tiffany with the blood on her sneakers. She broke down and changed her story. She says Jack attacked her brother, and Plekowski hit him with the urn in self defense. She also says it was dark, and she didn't realize Jack was badly hurt, otherwise she would have called an ambulance right away."

"So what's going to happen now?"

"Plekowski will be charged with breaking and entering, and probably attempted murder. He's trying to make some sort of plea bargain right now. Tiffany—I'm not sure what she'll be charged with—that's up to the prosecutor."

"And Doris' son and his wife?"

"He's denying everything. He says he was just venting to his wife's cousin about Doris hanging onto her money, but he never expected him to try to kidnap her and kill her cousin. Of course, he can't explain how the cousin knew where Charlie lived, but between him and his lawyer, they can probably come up with some explanation."

"So he's going to get away with it?"

"I don't know. We have the cab driver's testimony. He heard the son threaten Doris the day he picked her up to go to the airport, but that may not be enough. I think the least we can expect out of this is; we've caught the kidnapper and we've got him on the murder charges and attacking you. You're totally cleared of any complicity in your ex-husband's attack. Tiffany and her brother are going to face charges, plus we broke up a major drug ring. Kate, I know you thought I wasn't taking your concerns seriously, but we've been working on this drug case for the last year. And Walter Moore is still on my radar. His wife is a nice lady—she didn't deserve the treatment she got from him."

"And you didn't say one word to me about Walter."

"We were in the middle of an undercover operation. Besides, given your history, I was confident you could take care of yourself. I did try to warn you."

Yes, he had, and I ignored it, choosing instead to believe that Sam was jealous of Walter. How stupid could one woman get?

Chapter 33

"Kate, I've got something to tell you."

That evening, Doris had returned and she and I were eating dinner. She was complaining that the pot roast wasn't up to her usual standard. I couldn't see what the problem was—it tasted great to me.

"Did you wonder where I was today?"

"Yes, but you don't have to tell me if you don't want to."

"First of all, I had to see a lawyer about changing my will. I got that taken care of. Then I called my son to tell him he was specifically excluded, and wasn't getting a penny from my estate."

"So you think that you're safe from him now?"

"I do. He started to make excuses, said his wife's cousin thought up the whole scheme by himself. I refused to listen. I doubt he's given up entirely on getting some of the money, but as things stand, if anything happens to me, he gets nothing."

She paused to take a breath and went on, "I also talked to the lawyer about Charlie's estate. He left everything to me, and there's quite a bit of money. I don't feel right about having it. I've been thinking and thinking of what to do with it." She broke off and dabbed at her eyes. "Anyway, I don't want the money, but I want something good to come out of this. The lawyer suggested I set up a charitable trust, so Charlie's money can go to helping people." She looked at me. "What do you think, Kate?"

"I think it's a wonderful idea."

"The high school needs a new gym."

"You could name it for Charlie."

Her eyes filled with tears. "I think he'd like that."

I kissed her wrinkled cheek. "Charlie would be proud of you. I'd be honored to help"

Ellie called. "Mom, it's all over TV and the newspapers. They're saying the man they arrested at your house is the one who attacked Dad. He's Tiffany's brother, and she was there when he did it. The two of them just left Dad there, bleeding on the floor. If you hadn't come home when you did, the doctors said he could have died."

Suddenly I had changed from being the main suspect in a plot to kill my ex-husband, to his savior. I felt deeply sorry for Ellie. She was slowly realizing that her father had lied to her about his supposed amnesia.

"He's definitely going to divorce her. She's moved out and he's just waiting for the police to finish questioning her."

If she doesn't land in jail first, I thought.

Chapter 34

Margaret was finally out of the hospital and Doris and I were on our way to see her. Since she couldn't negotiate stairs and had difficulty moving around her small apartment on her crutches, the four of us— Stephen, Frank, Doris and me, with help from Rose and Enid, were going to take care of her and Louis until she could manage alone.

I planned to drop Doris off at the apartment building, and drive to the library to work my four hour shift. We had brought groceries with us. Doris was going to cook a few meals for Margaret that she could easily re-heat. I would pick Doris up after my shift ended and drive her home.

All the parking spaces on Margaret's street were filled. I had to double-park in order to carry the groceries upstairs. I rushed back down before I got a ticket, then took off for the library. Doris called before my shift ended. "The parking's filled up on both sides of the street. You can't even double-park. I'll meet you at the theater parking lot instead. It's only two blocks away. I'll take the short cut through the alley."

I was a few minutes late leaving the library. Traffic was heavy going through town, and I worried that Doris would already be at the theater waiting for me. I finally reached my turn and crossed the intersection. The theater parking lot was filled with the flashing, blue lights of police cars. An ambulance was parked at an angle, its rear doors wide open. There was no sign of Doris.

I pulled into the lot, ignoring the upraised hand of the officer put there to control traffic. I saw a man being questioned by one of the officers. In the distance, next to the ambulance, I spotted a familiar face. I left the car where it was and ran towards him, "Sam, have you seen Doris?"

I nearly fell as I stepped into one of the ruts that littered the surface. Sam caught me and held me upright. I frantically scanned the parking area. "I was supposed to meet her here. Have you seen her?"

"I'm all right, honey."

I looked around.

"I'm here in the ambulance."

Doris was sitting up on a stretcher holding her elbow against her body. She was pale, but otherwise looked unhurt.

I ran over to her, "What happened? I'm so sorry I was late. Traffic was terrible."

Sam came behind me, a comforting presence. "Take a breath, Kate. Doris is fine—a skinned elbow is all. She's going to have a doozy of a bruise, but nothing else. She's very lucky."

My legs refused to hold me. I sat down abruptly on the back step of the ambulance. How could I have let her walk back to the theater by herself in heavy, rush hour traffic? I should have told her to wait at Margaret's apartment until I got there.

Sam sat down next to me, and put his arm around my shoulder. I leaned into him. He felt good—warm and safe. I hurriedly pulled away and sat upright. Sam dropped his arm.

"They're taking Doris to the hospital to be checked out. Why don't you ride with her? Give me your keys. I'll drive your car and meet you there"

Sam and I were sitting opposite each other in the emergency room waiting area. Doris had been taken away on a stretcher, protesting vociferously. I heard her voice trailing back from the corridor. "There's no need for all this fuss, nothing wrong with me but a little bruise. I'm ready to go home."

I looked at Sam. "What really happened? All Doris said was she was almost hit by a car."

"Which didn't stop," he said quietly.

"Are you saying it wasn't an accident?"

"She had the light to cross the street and had just stepped out into the crosswalk when a car came around the corner and aimed right for her. If our witness hadn't had extremely swift reflexes, the car would have hit her. As it was, he grabbed her by the scruff of her neck, and pulled her out of its path. They both fell back onto the sidewalk, which is where she got the scraped elbow."

"But who could have done it? Her kidnapper is in custody."

Sam sighed. "I was never comfortable with Margaret Adams' fall at the theater. I accepted it as an accident because there didn't seem to be a motive for it to be anything else."

"Sam, when Frank and I were telling you what happened that day, I knew something wasn't right, but I couldn't remember what it was. When Frank and I found Margaret, the basement door was closed and the light off. We talked to Margaret at the hospital, and she told us the reason she went over to the door was because the light was on, and the door open. She was certain that she and Stephen had turned off the lights the night before."

"So someone else had to have been there, and that someone was the one who turned off the light and closed the door. Probably hoping she wouldn't be found for some time."

"If I hadn't needed a clean apron for the show, she could have lain there for two, or even three days."

Sam nodded slowly, his mind working.

"But why? Who could possibly want to hurt Margaret?"

"I don't think it was Margaret they wanted. Have you noticed how much she and Doris look alike? Maybe not to people who know them, but if you just had a description...."

"But the kidnapper is in custody now."

"Kate, it couldn't have been Dee. We had him under surveillance, and he was nowhere near the theater that Sunday."

"Then that means...?"

"Someone else is out there, and Doris is still in danger."

Chapter 35

Doris was furious when we told her. "I don't care what you think. I'm not hiding out again. I'm going home with Kate."

"But, Doris, if you go back to the house, you'll put Kate in danger, too," Sam pointed out.

"And Enid and Rose," I added.

She looked at us both, pursed her lips and sighed. "Where do you want me to go this time?"

I had the perfect solution.

Later, as Sam was driving me home, I asked, "Doris will be safe there, won't she?"

"Pamela Moore has the apartment across from Margaret and she's agreed to let a policewoman stay at her place. They're the only two apartments on that landing, so it's easy to secure. Margaret needs someone to take care of her, and Doris will be in her element doing that. What could be better?"

"You don't think whoever tried to run her down followed her from Margaret's apartment?"

"Our witness says the car was going across the intersection then suddenly swerved, and turned right instead. I think it was a crime of opportunity. The driver was going about his business when he spotted her and decided to take a chance."

Sam pulled into the alley behind the house and parked my car. I asked him how he was getting home.

"What if I sleep on your couch again, just until I can get some security arrangements set up?"

"Sam, I appreciate what you did tonight, but I don't need to be looked after. I'm perfectly capable of taking care of myself."

"Tiffany had keys to the back door and the third floor apartment. Who knows how many others are floating around out there?"

"Nevertheless, I don't want you or any other law enforcement officer staying at my apartment."

He glared at me. The familiar pulse throbbed in his jaw. He nodded a tight-lipped acquiescence. He walked me to the back entrance and waited until I went up the stairs and opened my door. I looked out the kitchen window and saw him talking on his cell phone. A few minutes later, his SUV pulled onto the parking pad next to my car. The red-headed girlfriend got out. They briefly hugged, switched places, and Sam drove down the alley and out of sight.

Chapter 36

I was living alone again. I missed Doris. Martha was the conduit by which the two way messages flowed, but they were of the everyday variety: how are you doing? are you eating enough? and more frequently, is Digger eating enough? Enid and Rose checked on me daily and Rose, armed with her trusty skillet, came down the back stairs with me when Digger needed to go out after dark.

A couple of weeks went by. I heard nothing from Sam. I worked my shift at the library, took Digger for his walks, but all the time my mind was churning, going over the events of the past few weeks.

Finally, I decided to call Walter.

"Walter, would you meet me at Luigi's this evening?"

Would he? He was ecstatic.

"I knew it wouldn't last with the police detective. I was going to call you anyway. Did you know he has a new girlfriend, someone young enough to be his daughter?"

I almost said there's a lot of that going around.

"I'll pick you up at seven."

"Don't bother. I'll meet you there."

This was almost a re-run of my first date with Walter, except he was already seated when I arrived. He was at the same table as before and had already ordered wine and dinner.

He leaned in close and tried to grab my hand. "You look beautiful this evening, Kate. You've done something different to your hair. I like it."

I moved my hand away. "This isn't a social occasion Walter. I have some questions for you."

I saw that little flare in his eyes, but he smiled agreeably and said, "Anything, Kate. Ask away."

"The first time we went out, how did you know where I lived?"

"You told me."

"No, I didn't."

"Then your daughter must have said something when she came into the dental office. Yes, I'm sure she did. She told me you lived in the yellow Victorian, close to the old library."

"And did she also tell you about Doris living with me?"

He paused. "What is this, Kate? I thought we were going to enjoy a nice dinner."

"No, it's strictly business, Walter."

I looked up as Luigi led a group of people into the dining room. One of them was the young police officer who had interrogated me during my first circle of hell. Then came Sam's redheaded girlfriend, and to round out the party nicely, Sam himself, who scowled as soon as he caught sight of me.

I ignored him and got back to Walter. "You never actually met my room-mate, Doris, until the day we were breaking down the set at the theater, did you? You had a description of her, but it was vague—old lady, worked at the theater. And you made a big mistake."

He leaned across the table as if to quiet me. I kept talking. "The day after the run of our play ended, you came backstage to invite me to dinner. That's when you saw Doris. I thought you were upset because I'd told you to stop bothering me. But it had nothing to do with me. You saw her and realized you'd pushed the wrong person down the stairs. But you didn't leave it there. When you saw her walking near the theater, you saw another opportunity and seized it. You were the one who tried to run her down."

He stood up abruptly, knocking over his chair. Out of the corner of my eye, I saw Sam rise.

Walter reached across the table, but Sam was already behind him. He put him in an arm-lock. Walter struggled to get free, but the young policeman appeared on his other side. He cuffed him. Walter was frantic, almost frothing at the mouth. "You stupid bitch, why did you have to poke your nose into something that doesn't concern you?"

Poor Luigi, by the time Walter was hauled off in a police car, he was so distraught, his Italian accent had disappeared entirely, and he was left with nothing but his native Hoosier. A bewildered waiter arrived at the table bearing the entrees Walter had ordered, and for once, I paid for the entire meal.

Chapter 37

I should have felt guilty for breaking up Sam's dinner party, but I didn't. He and the young detective left with Walter. Sam's girlfriend sat alone, with only a filled bread basket and a bottle of wine for company.

On his way out, a furious Sam said through clenched teeth, "I'll be back. Don't go anywhere."

I almost saluted.

"Hi, there."

I looked up to find Sam's girlfriend standing next to my table, grinning down at me. She had the bread basket in one hand, and the wine in the other.

"Mind if I join you? I hate to eat alone."

"Feel free."

I waved magnanimously at the two platters of steaming linguini sitting forlornly in the middle of the table. "Would you like to share? Looks as if my dinner companion isn't coming back anytime soon."

She sat. "I'm Mira. You must be Kate. My Dad's told me a lot about you. You're the one responsible for the spike in his blood pressure."

My mouth dropped open. "You're Sam's daughter?"

She laughed. "Well, I'm a little young to be his girlfriend, don't you think?"

I smiled weakly.

"I work in the DA's office in Cincinnati. I'm spending a couple of weeks with my Dad—not that I've seen much of him—but that's the way law enforcement goes and since I'm engaged to Kevin I'd better get used to it.

"Kevin?"

"You've met Kevin. He was the other officer who questioned you when your ex-husband was found unconscious in your apartment. We were supposed to have dinner with Dad tonight to celebrate the engagement, but it looks as if we've both been abandoned."

She poured two glasses of wine, pulled one of the plates over to her, and started eating. If I'd had any doubts about her parentage, they were entirely quelled. She inhaled her food just like Sam.

"Martha tells me you beat your husband with a golf club when you found him and his secretary having sex in his office. Is that true?"

"She was his personal assistant, not his secretary."

"Very personal—right?" She lifted her wine glass. "To marriage and Mister Right."

We toasted. Then Mira said, "When are you going to stop being mad at my Dad? He's a great guy if you'd only give him a chance."

By the time we were half way through the second bottle, Mira and I were best friends. I learned her mother didn't want her to marry anyone in law enforcement, but as Mira said, it's not as if she didn't know what she was getting into.

"Still, when I broke the news to her about Kevin, she was so angry I decided to take some vacation days and get out of town until she cooled down a little."

Mira was a force of nature. By the time we had totally killed the second bottle, I'd heard everything there was to tell about Sam. He and his wife had divorced when Mira was five, and her mother had remarried. Her stepfather was a patent attorney, which meant he kept regular hours.

"I'm fond of him, but Dad and I are real close. We think alike about almost everything. I can see why he's so stuck on you."

"Stuck on me? He can't stand me. We spend most of the time arguing."

Mira just laughed. I was about to debate my point when I felt a presence looming over me.

"Are you ready to leave?"

The question was a mere formality. Mira and I looked at each other, and started giggling. I stood, swaying slightly. Kevin hauled Mira out of her chair. "Come on, Sunshine, time to go."

We staggered out to Luigi's parking lot. Mira gave me a big hug. I hugged her back.

"Call me. Let's get drunk together again."

Sam took my car keys from my purse and opened the passenger side door. I stumbled into the car. Leaning back against the headrest, I told him, "I feel so relaxed."

"You're drunk," he said softly.

"I know but it only happens when I'm around a Williamson."

That seemed so funny, I couldn't stop laughing.

Sam helped me up the backstairs. I almost fell into the kitchen, but he guided me down the hallway and into the bedroom. I felt him take off my jacket and shoes. I collapsed onto the bed.

He left but was back a few minutes later. He came around the side of the bed and helped me up into a sitting position, supporting my head on his arm. I felt him slip a couple of pills into my mouth then hold a glass to my lips.

"Aspirin and water," he whispered. "It will help with the hangover in the morning."

I dutifully swallowed and collapsed back onto my pillow.

Sam covered me with the duvet. I thought I felt his lips brush my cheek. "Sleep tight."

And I did.

Chapter 38

I heard the shower run, smelled coffee and put my head under the covers. I was not ready to face Sam. Last time I'd overindulged, he had been drunk too, but I was all on my own with this one.

There was a soft rap at the door. "Are you ready for tea?"

I cautiously uncovered one eye. I could kill for a cup of tea.

"I have to go into the precinct, but don't think you're off the hook about last night."

I groaned. "Not now, please."

Sam sat on the edge of the bed, and slowly pulled the cover down until he could see all of my face. "I'm still angry with you. I'll give you the morning to recover, but I expect you down at the station at two."

I put my hand out. Sam put the cup into it and curled my fingers around the handle. "Two o' clock sharp."

We were sitting in the same room where Sam and Kevin had interrogated me after Jack had been discovered on my kitchen floor with his skull practically cracked open. The room was still cramped and depressing, and the smell was no better, but at least this time I wasn't the suspect.

The soft, caring Sam had disappeared. He had on his interrogation face.

"From what I gather, last night you accused Walter Moore of not only pushing Margaret Adams down the basement steps at the theater, but also of trying to run Doris down with his SUV. Do you have any proof of that?"

"Not proof exactly."

"Then what?"

"I had a feeling."

He gave an exasperated sigh.

"I know—I know, but there were little things that didn't add up. Separately, they didn't amount to much, but when I put them together, there seemed to be a pattern."

"And you couldn't have called me and shared your concerns?"

I looked at him and raised an eyebrow. He dropped his eyes, and pretended to study his notes.

"The first time Walter asked me out, he knew where I lived without my telling him. He said my daughter had given him my address when she came into the dental office, and I suppose that's possible. But then I wondered why she would do that and what else had she told him? So I asked if she had mentioned that Doris lived with me. That got a huge reaction. I could tell he was angry and nervous at the same time."

"Kate, we were already putting a case together against Moore. You damn near blew it for us. Luckily, we have enough to hold him on other charges. Otherwise, we'd be looking for a safe place to hide you. He's a dangerous man."

"Maybe, if you called once in a while I would have known that and backed off. It's called communication, Sam."

He glared at me across the table. I glared back.

"Is that it? Or do you have any more feelings?" The way he spat out the word—it was dripping with sarcasm.

"There's more. You've already mentioned that Margaret and Doris look alike, and to somebody who's never seen either before, they could be mistaken for one another. That Sunday when we were breaking down the set at the theater, Walter came by to invite me to dinner. I had just found out that he had been abusive to his ex-wife, so I was less than polite. He backed away from me, looking almost panic-stricken. I thought it was because I threatened him with you, but it wasn't. Doris was there, and I think when Walter saw her, he realized that he'd pushed the wrong person down the stairs. From there, it's hardly a jump to accusing him of trying to run her down, which I did."

Sam dropped his face into his hands and massaged it vigorously.

He raised his head. "What exactly did you hope to accomplish by accusing him?"

"I thought he might let something slip, or at the least, know that someone was watching him, and he would leave Doris alone. After all, he does think I'm dating a policeman."

Though, I thought, *that's no longer valid because Walter thought Sam's daughter was his new girlfriend.*

"We were building another case entirely, around Moore. The back-pack that Tiffany dropped the night you ran into her at the house had dozens of prescriptions for Vicodin and other drugs, in a bunch of false names. Moore wrote the prescriptions, and Plekowski went to different pharmacies and used fake ID's to pick them up. Then Plekowski sold the drugs out of the apartment in your house, and shared the proceeds with Walter."

"So that's why Mrs. Turner said there were always people coming and going from the backstairs."

Sam nodded. "And why the lights were always burnt out. So no-one could identify them."

"But I don't understand how Tiffany's brother, Walter, and the kidnapper tie in together."

"Walter was Tiffany's dentist."

That figured. She probably started going to him when she married Jack.

"She told him her brother was moving to Shelbyville and she was trying to find a job for him. Tiffany's the one who rented the apartment. Though, at that time she didn't know you were living there. Walter said he would like to meet Plekowski. He did, and proposed the drug scheme to him. Wayne's not the brightest and agreed. At this point, we're not sure if Tiffany knew anything about the drugs or not, though it's hard to believe she didn't figure it out. After your neighbor Rose, almost caught Plekowski trying to get into your apartment, he was scared that she'd recognized him, so decided to get out of Shelbyville. He contacted Johnny Dee, with whom he had served time at one point and hid out in his motel room."

"So Walter and Johnny Dee weren't connected except indirectly through Tiffany's brother? But why would Walter try to kill Doris?"

"We've been watching Walter for some time. He's a real lowlife, with a heavy gambling problem. He spends a lot of time at the horse track out on I-74. He ran through all of his wife's money and put her in the hospital a few times. When she finally left him, she had to get a restraining order because he was stalking her."

Now I was really confused. "How did the kidnapper know that Doris was living in Shelbyville?"

"He didn't. He was frantic when he lost her at the airport. After all, he had just committed two murders. He saw the funeral information in the local paper and drove up to Wadesboro that day to see if she would be at the service."

"But I was certain we had lost him. We took back roads all the way to I-65."

"He saw Frank's Shelby County license plate. That's why he was in Shelbyville the day you saw him. It was sheer luck—or bad luck for you—that he ran into you."

Sam continued. "When Dee saw you outside the bakery, he was worried you would go to the police. He decided to stay out of Shelbyville and that's when he asked Plekowski to find out where you and Doris lived."

"And Plekowski asked Walter. So that's why Walter asked Ellie where I lived. And that's why he asked me out."

"Well that, and the fact that he was broke and needed another..." he stopped abruptly.

"Cash cow?" I finished for him.

Sam looked slightly ashamed, but he plowed on. "When Walter went to the theater on opening night, he saw Doris' name listed on the program as assistant costumer. After you turned down another date with him, he started hanging around the theater, hoping that somebody would let slip Doris' whereabouts. He saw Margaret go into the theater that Sunday, mistook her for Doris, and followed her. After turning on the lights in the basement to lure her over to the door, he pushed her down the stairs. His mistake was turning off the light and closing the door. But for that, it would have looked like an accident."

"Then why did Johnny Dee come to my apartment if he thought Walter had taken care of her?"

"Because when Dee tried to get information at the hospital about Doris' condition, he was told she was not a patient there. He desperately needed the money her son was going to pay him to buy into the meth trade. Walter must have told him where you lived."

I thought about this for a minute then asked, "Once Dee was in custody, why did Walter try to run Doris down?"

"Because he was desperate for money, too. With Plekowski in hiding, Walter's share of the drug trade was cut off. After Dee was arrested, Walter immediately contacted Doris' son and offered to pick up where Dee left off. We think he was trying to buy into the meth trade in Dee's place."

I had one more question. "Why did Tiffany's brother come back to the house? He must have known you were looking for him."

"When we raided Dee's motel room, Plekowski had nowhere else to go. He slipped in through the back door, not knowing Mrs. Turner was watching for him."

"So you really didn't need my help. You had everything figured after all."

"Pretty much. Now we have to prove everything."

Chapter 39

I went home in a chastened mood. My brilliant deductions had been nothing but wild guesses. I couldn't blame Sam for being angry with me. As he pointed out, I could have totally blown his case for him. Maybe he was right and I should leave detecting to the professionals.

But a little voice in the back of my mind said that I was the one who'd brought Doris home. I was the one who, in a way, caught Dee for Sam. I was the one who alerted Sam after Doris left. And if I ever saw Sam again, which after today I doubted, I would point all that out to him.

But maybe I wouldn't, because the little voice told me that Sam already knew about Dee and had him under surveillance because he was working on his big drug case. I did find out about the connection between Tiffany and Plekowski which solved Jack's attack. At least that was mine.

On the plus side, Doris was safe—all the bad guys were in jail and according to Sam, not getting out for some time. Now she could come home.

She was thrilled, but torn. "Kate, who's going to take care of Margaret? And Louis? She's not well enough to manage on her own yet."

Margaret spoke up. "That's not a problem, Doris. Frank comes by often." Did I detect a faint blush when she spoke his name? "And Pamela stops in after she gets home from work."

She'd hardly got the words out when there was a soft knock at the door. Pamela poked her head in. "Oh, you have company. I'll come back later." Then she saw it was me, and a big smile lit up her face. She almost danced into Margaret's living room. "Kate, did you hear Walter's been arrested?"

She laughed. "Maybe now I can have a normal life instead of always looking over my shoulder."

Doris gave her a big hug. "You'll do fine, my love."

Margaret beamed. "Louis and I will be fine too."

"Well, there's plenty of casseroles in the freezer, and Frank just brought by the groceries I asked for. I'll come over tomorrow, and cook some more for you. Why don't you and Pamela sit down and eat that lasagna I made?"

As soon as Doris was sure that no one was going to starve before her next visit, she was ready to leave. She handed me a large parcel. "You take that and I'll carry my little bag."

When we got back to my apartment, I found that Frank had dropped off a plush bed for Digger, plenty big enough for him to stretch out and sleep. Doris opened her parcel and brought out a fluffy pillow that fit the bed exactly and an embroidered quilt with Digger's name splashed across the front.

He hopped right in. Doris covered him with his quilt and he promptly fell asleep. I felt abandoned until, at some point in the night, Digger woke me by crawling up on the bed and I fell back to sleep to the sound of his gentle snores.

Chapter 40

Ellie called. She sounded nervous. "Mom, Dad wants to talk to you. He wants you to meet him at the office."

"Why? What can he possibly have to say to me?"

"He wants to explain everything."

Poor Ellie, she had never really accepted the divorce, but I didn't want to raise any false hope. "Ellie, I have no desire to discuss anything with your father."

"Please, Mom. What could it hurt to just hear him out?"

She sounded on the verge of tears. I had a few questions of my own for Jack. Reluctantly, I agreed to see him.

Going back into his office was an unsettling experience. I hadn't been there since the day I was hauled off to jail for attacking him with his golf club. An older woman stood at a file cabinet, with a bunch of papers in her hand. Evidently, Tiffany had already been replaced.

"Can I help you?"

I was about to answer, when Jack came out of the inner office. His face lit up when he saw me. "Kate, you came."

He looked older, drawn. His head had been shaved when he was in the hospital, and the hair growing in was patchy and gray. The suntan was gone. He had lost weight, and his face was sagging. No young Lothario now, he looked at least ten years older than the last time I'd seen him.

"Let's go in my office." He turned to the woman and barked out, "No calls. We don't want to be disturbed."

She gave him a hostile look.

The office was the same as I remembered, except the golf clubs were gone. Jack pulled the client chair closer to the side of the desk and went to close the door.

"Leave it open, Jack. I'm not staying long."

I sat, put my purse on the floor, crossed my legs and leaned back. "Ellie says you want to talk to me?"

He smiled and tried to take my hand. I pulled away from him.

"Kate, I know I made a huge mistake in divorcing you."

"Actually, Jack, I divorced you, for adultery, remember? And that wasn't the only mistake you made."

He shrugged his shoulders as if to say, that's all in the past now.

"I want you to know Tiffany and I are finished. She's already moved out."

He looked at me expectantly. I was silent. He waited about five beats for my response. Then, getting none, said, "Have you ever thought we could start over…go back to the way we were?"

"What? Remarry?"

"Exactly, Kate; we had a good marriage. We could have that again."

I was speechless. Did Jack really think I was that stupid?

His voice became more urgent, "Kate, it was a mid-life crisis. Can't you understand that?"

I watched his face closely. "Answer this, Jack; how long did you think it was me who attacked you the night you were almost killed?"

He was thinking about lying. I could see the decision process move across his face. Then he sighed. "Until just before they moved me out of ICU at the hospital. I really did have amnesia those first few days. I couldn't remember anything about that night."

"But when I came to see you in your hospital room, you'd recovered your memory, and yet you still lied to me. Why? Why didn't you tell the police what happened?"

He squirmed uncomfortably. "I had to think it through before I said anything."

"Why not just tell the truth?"

"Well, it was damned embarrassing..." he broke off.

"Because it was Tiffany who hit you with my urn that night, not her brother."

It was a statement not a question.

He pushed his chair back and stood, "I came home early one Thursday from a meeting and she wasn't there. When she came in she was shocked to see me. She told me she'd run out to get something from the store, but she didn't bring anything back with her. I knew she was lying."

He started pacing. "I really didn't think she would cheat on me but..."

"You wanted to be sure."

He nodded. "The next week I told her I had another meeting. I waited down the street, and watched the house. Sure enough, she came out of the driveway and drove past me. I followed her to your place, though I didn't know you lived there then," he added hastily. "She went up a flight of stairs in the back of the house. A man was opening the door to an apartment. She grabbed his arm, but he pulled away and went in. She followed him, and they started to argue. I heard her say—*don't do it, if you get caught you'll go back inside*—that's when the man turned and saw me. He tried to push past and get out the door, but I held onto him, and that's all I remembered until I woke up in the hospital."

"So how do you know it was Tiffany who hit you over the head with the urn, not the brother?"

"I heard someone behind me while we were struggling, and smelled perfume. I recognized it. I had bought it for her on our honeymoon."

"And how could you tell anyone?" I said softly, "You had broken up a thirty year marriage for this woman, and she'd almost killed you to protect her drug-dealing brother?"

"I knew you'd understand, Kate. After all the bad publicity you put me through when we divorced, I couldn't go through that again."

"And besides, Ellie tells me you're thinking of running for a seat on the city council. It wouldn't look good for you to have a felon for a brother-in-law."

He sat down and tried to take my hand again. "Kate, we can still make it work. After all, we both made mistakes. You dated that drug-dealing dentist of mine."

"But that was after the divorce, and it was hardly an affair."

He ignored me. "Ellie says you only went out with him twice."

"Actually, it was three times."

"But he was the only one you dated."

"No, he wasn't."

"There was someone else?"

I nodded.

"But it wasn't serious? You didn't...?"

"I did."

There was a sharp intake of breath. Jack bowed his head for a few moments. He looked up at me. "It's all right, Kate, I forgive you. We'll forget this and never talk of it again."

I took a deep breath, fighting the urge to collapse into helpless laughter. The idiot actually thought I needed his forgiveness. I picked up my purse and headed for the door.

He came around the desk to stop me. "Kate, please wait."

I paused in front of him. "Jack, understand this, there is absolutely no chance of a reconciliation. Not because you had an affair. Not because you let the police, and what is worse, our daughter, believe that I had attacked you, just so you could save face. But because you're a pathetic, pompous bore and my life is so much better without you. Now get out of my way."

He stood for a moment. An angry flush suffused his face. He turned, forgot about the door being open, and ran head first into the edge of it. I heard a crack as his nose made contact. The blood spurted out, pouring down the front of his shirt.

He stood there with his hand to his nose. Blood trickled through his fingers, "Oh damn it! Damn it that hurts."

I finally lost control. The laughter poured out of me and I couldn't stop it. I laughed so hard my stomach hurt and tears poured down my face. Jack stared at me, dumbfounded

I went past him into the outer office. Jack's new secretary was standing next to the door.

She was laughing too. She handed me a wad of tissues. "Karma's a bitch, wouldn't you say, Mrs. Conley?"

I mopped my eyes and left, still laughing.

Chapter 41

I was at the library the next morning, shelving a bottom row of books, when I saw a familiar pair of legs standing to the right of me. Another pair, not so familiar, was to my left. I looked up, took the proffered hand and hauled myself to my feet.

Sam looked nervous. "Is there somewhere we could talk in private?"

I glanced at Sebastian who was working at the other end of the stacks. "Is it all right if the detectives and I use the break room for a few minutes?"

He nodded his head. "Sure, nobody's in there right now."

I ushered Sam and his cohort, Kevin, into the room and closed the door behind us.

Sam cleared his throat. "I hope you don't mind us coming to your place of business. We stopped by the apartment and Doris told us you were at work."

Kevin broke in, "We have some news you might want to hear and Sam…" He stopped as Sam sent him a warning look.

Sam started. "Walter Moore, Dee, and Plekowski have all confessed. Each blames the other, but we have a pretty solid case against all three. With Moore and Dee's testimony, we can get Doris' son and his wife on conspiracy to commit murder. The son broke first and implicated his wife. She says it was all his idea, that she knew nothing about the plot. Dee says both of them were in on it."

"So you see, Kate," he went on, "we police really can solve our own cases without the help of happy amateurs."

"But didn't this happy amateur solve the mystery of the body lying on my kitchen floor?" I asked sweetly. "After all, I was the one who found the connection between Jack, Tiffany, and her brother. Without my help you would never have solved the case. You couldn't see any further than the ex-wife."

Sam leaned across the table, laser eyes boring into mine. "I'll grant you that, but we were the ones who confirmed your alibi."

"After I asked you if there were street cameras you could check."

His jaw started throbbing. "Your meddling put you in some damned dangerous situations, Kate."

"Meddling?"

Kevin stopped us. "Wait a minute, Sam. We didn't come to argue, remember?"

Sam glared at him. Kevin fell silent.

"You know, Martha was at the emergency room last night with an accident victim. She ran into your former husband. He'd broken his nose. Had you heard anything about it?"

"I did see him yesterday." I said cautiously. "He wanted to talk to me about getting back together."

"You mean remarrying?"

"Yes."

"And?"

"I told him about a little indiscretion I had committed after the divorce."

Sam almost choked. "And the reconciliation was off?"

"On the contrary, he forgave me."

"Ah, and that's when the nose was broken?"

"Precisely."

"You know," said Kevin, "I almost feel sorry for the poor bastard. His first wife chases him with a golf club and puts him in the emergency room. His second wife breaks an urn over his head and damn near kills him." He started to laugh and Sam joined in. "When he tries to reconcile with wife number one," by now, tears were running down his face, "she breaks his nose."

He gave an almighty guffaw, and they were both pounding on the table, unable to get out another word.

"He walked into a door," I almost yelled. "If you don't believe me, ask his secretary. She saw the whole thing."

The door creaked open. An anxious Sebastian peered in, Frank and Clarice crowding behind him.

"Do you need any help in here?"

Sam wiped his eyes. "No, we're fine. If you could give us a few more minutes...?"

With a worried look, Sebastian closed the door. Kevin looked meaningfully at Sam.

Sam's ears turned bright red. He cleared his throat again. "Kate, I was wondering... I mean, I actually came by to ask..."

Finally, he blurted out, "Would you go to dinner with me?"

"Dinner with you? Why?"

"Well, I'd call it a date."

"Why would I want to date you, Sam?"

He looked at me uncertainly. "You don't?"

"If someone asks me out, I expect it to be without the schoolboy sniggering. If you will excuse me, I have to get back to work."

I thought I'd handled the situation with dignity, but my exit was totally ruined by Clarice. She was down on one knee, looking through the keyhole. When I opened the door and swept out, I tripped over her and we both ended up flat on our backs.

Sam hurried over and extended his hand to help me. I pushed it away and picked myself up off the floor.

As I walked away, I heard Kevin say, "He walked into a door." And they exploded again into helpless laughter. *It would be a cold day in hell,* I told myself, *before I ever dated Detective Sam Williamson.*

Chapter 42

When I got back from the library, Doris was in the kitchen pulling a batch of scones out of the oven. She had made tiny, smoked salmon and cucumber sandwiches and was using the silver tea service and my best bone china cups and plates.

"Doris, why are we so fancy today?"

"I've got an announcement to make."

I was about to ask her what it was and why she was acting so mysteriously when Enid and Rose knocked at the door. They were carrying a bottle of champagne and a jug of orange juice.

Rose waved the champagne. "We thought we'd have some mimosas with our tea."

When we had our glasses filled, Doris raised hers. "Here's to our new, permanent home."

Enid, Rose and I looked at each other in bewilderment.

"Remember when our landlord called and you made me talk to him?"

I did. He and Doris had been on the phone for almost an hour.

"He was very upset about the drug raid, and the fact that the doors had been kicked in again just after he had them fixed."

She paused. She was enjoying our confusion.

"He told me he was sorry he ever bought the house, so I said if we could agree on a fair price, I might be willing to take it off his hands.

Rose, Enid and I looked at each other, wondering what was going to come next.

"And since we'd had drug raids, attempted murder, and a tenant attacked by a crazed, drug lord, the price was reasonable and he was glad to unload it, even at a loss."

"But, Doris, you can't afford a house like this."

I thought of the vintage suitcase which seemed to contain a few housedresses and a couple of aprons, her thrifty shopping, the sugar packets she collected off restaurant tables and ended up saying lamely, "You're always so careful with money."

"That's why I have so much. Never saw no sense in wasting it. Otis and I were born in the Depression when every penny counted. We never were ones for a big show. We bought land when it was cheap, and added to it when our neighbors were selling off. We did all right for ourselves."

She raised her glass. "Let's drink our mim things and I'll tell you what I've got planned for us."

Doris had it all worked out. Enid and Rose were to move to the top apartment.

"That way," she said, "you can use the attic for your separate studios. The light is good and there's plenty of space. We can remodel the old carriage house, turn it into a garage and have room for three cars. Kate can keep this apartment, and I'll take the one downstairs."

She saw the startled look on my face. "You might need a little more privacy one of these days when you start dating again."

I almost choked on my mimosa. "Who says I'll be dating? I'm done with all that."

Enid, Rose and Doris stood, raised their glasses, and said in unison, "Methinks, the lady doth protest too much."

They were right. I did protest too much. There was a knock at the back door the next morning. A shamefaced Sam stood there with a bunch of flowers in his hand. His ears were bright red again.

He blurted out, "Look, I want to apologize if I gave the impression I thought you had broken your ex-husband's nose. Martha questioned him at the hospital, and he said it was your fault that it happened. When she pressed him, he admitted he walked into the door, but said you were the one who insisted it be left open."

"So are the flowers by way of apology, Sam?"

"No, yesterday I asked you out on a date. Now I'm asking you again, but this time I'm going to do it properly."

He tried to hand me the flowers. I was silent. I didn't know if I should let him off that easily.

"Kate, when we first met, we both got off on the wrong foot."

"Well, yes. You arrested me for attacking my ex-husband."

"No, I meant…." His face became beet red and he couldn't get the words out.

I took pity on him. "Sam, if you're talking about that night in your apartment, we were both drunk. I thought we were going to forget it ever happened."

"I can't, Kate. I should never have …"

I sighed, "Well, ask me out and get it over with."

He opened his mouth again but no words came out.

"Are you still going to ask me?"

Sam managed to choke out, "Yes."

I took the flowers from him. "I'll think about it."

Chapter 43

Enid's art exhibit was opening that night in Fountain Square. The show was in the same venue that Rose's had been. The wine was as bad as before and Doris took it upon herself to interpret the works once again.

The hit of the show, which had crowds around it all night and which sold almost as soon as the doors opened, was a painting of a woman. She was crouched in the bottom corner of the canvas, a figure portraying utter despair. Enid had smashed my wedding ring into pieces and placed them off center. From the broken ring, crystal drops cascaded down into the murk below. There were tiny crystals on the woman's face, as if the tears dripping from the wedding ring had splashed onto her. The name of the painting was on the card to the right. "Trust Betrayed."

The door opened, letting in a blast of cold night air. I looked around. It was Frank pushing Margaret's wheelchair. Behind them, Stephen held the door for Sebastian and Pamela. Clarice came in with Sylvia, who immediately started scanning the room. Another blind date, I figured.

As I made my way towards them, the door opened again. This time it was Mira, with Kevin and Martha. Sam wasn't among the group.

My disappointment must have shown on my face because Martha laughed, "He's finding a parking space, Kate. He'll be here soon."

Sure enough, I felt another blast of cold air. I turned to see Sam standing in the doorway. He saw me and started making his way through the crowd toward me.

He cleared his throat. "You probably have dinner plans for later, don't you?"

"I do. After the show is over, we always meet at the Greek restaurant down the street. Why don't you come with me?"

He covered my hand with his and smiled down at me. He really was an amazingly handsome man with his silver gray hair and vivid blue eyes. "I'd love that, Kate."

I made my decision. "Sam, would you get me a glass of wine. I have a quick phone call I have to make."

I waited until he made his way toward the wine table, sought out a quiet corner, took out my phone and dialed.

"Mom, this is Kate. I'm sorry to call so late but there's something I should have told you a long time ago."

The End

ABOUT THE AUTHOR

 Trisha Durrant was raised in post-war Britain. After seeing an ad in the *London Times*, which said, 'Come to the sun-drenched desert of Arizona,' she immediately decided to emigrate. In her defense, it was raining at the time and she was an out of work actor who was tired of waiting on tables. Now four children, eight grand-children, many homes and too many cats to enumerate later, she lives in beautiful Asheville, North Carolina, with her remaining cat Monty, nicknamed "The Monster." *Almost Abducted* is the first book in her new Kate and Doris Mystery series.

www.ingramcontent.com/pod-product-compliance
Lightning Source LLC
Chambersburg PA
CBHW020328260626
47156CB00004B/1430